John Rankine was born in Hawarden and educated at Chester Grammar School and Manchester University, where he obtained a BA degree in English and Psychology. He has a wide appeal as a Science Fiction writer and has written both series and short stories, one of which was adapted for one of televisions 'Out of the Unknown' series.

John Rankine is married with four children and lives in Wallasey, Cheshire, where he is a headmaster.

Also available in this Space 1999 series:

BREAKAWAY by E. C. Tubb
MOON ODYSSEY by John Rankine
THE SPACE GUARDIANS by Brian Ball
COLLISION COURSE by E. C. Tubb
LUNAR ATTACK by John Rankine

John Rankine

Space 1999:
Astral Quest

Futura Publications Limited
An Orbit Book

An Orbit Book

First published in Great Britain in 1975
by Futura Publications Limited
Warner Road, London SE5

Series format and television play scripts
Copyright © ITC – Incorporated Television
Company Limited 1975

This novelization copyright © John Rankine 1975

This book is based on scripts from the television
series SPACE 1999

This book is sold subject to the condition
that it shall not, by way of trade or
otherwise, be lent, re-sold, hired out or
otherwise circulated without the publisher's
prior consent in any form of binding or
cover other than that in which it is
published and without a similar condition
including this condition being imposed on the
subsequent purchaser.

ISBN: 0 8600 7878 7
Printed in Great Britain by
Hazell Watson & Viney Ltd
Aylesbury, Bucks

Futura Publications Limited
Warner Road, London SE5

CHAPTER ONE

John Koenig, Commander of Moon Base Alpha, considered that his people must have worked the longest duty stint ever recorded in the annals of the Space Service. If there was any truth in the old line that living was struggling and the prudent man learned to like it, they had qualified by a big margin . . . at least on the struggling bit.

For that matter, they were making out on the second item. Looking around the sprawling complex, he found that morale was still high. The selectors who had staffed the base had done a good job.

Unimaginable distance now separated them from their homes on Earth. As the Moon fled on, probing beams searched in all directions for a new Earth. Round the clock, Computer sifted and processed the data. Negative. Negative.

The Command Office was as quiet as a vault and Koenig looked at his time disc. He had sat long at his desk. The watch in Main Mission must have changed. Checking it by looking through his observation port, he could see that it was so. Paul Morrow, the top hand of the executive staff was back at his control console and Sandra Benes was moving elegantly to the communications slot.

On his desk top, Koenig saw a litter of calculations and moodily gathered the slips in a bunch for the trash can. All the theory in the world was so much crap against one observed fact.

He had taken the crude statistic of 10^{20} for a measure of the stars within range of their telescopes. From there, he had allowed himself one in a thousand with a planetary system. Of those, he gave a chance of conditions necessary to life at one in a thousand against. So he was still left with 10^{14}. Refining again, he had got down to 10^{11} with an atmosphere. Knocking expectation with a club, he had to concede that somewhere there had to be a hundred million planets where life had actually got up a little steam. And he only wanted one.

As he used his comlock to open the hatch into Main Mission

another thought struck him. Out of all that rag bag, there would be many civilisations so advanced that he and his people would look like aborigines. It was too early in the morning to chase that one to its hole and stare at it. He stretched wearily and moved slowly down the steps to the floor of the operations area and joined Paul Morrow at his console.

'Any problems, Paul?'

'The universe sleeps.'

It reminded Koenig that it had been a long and busy day. 'It knows a good thing. I'm more than ready to join it.'

'Then I'll say good night, Commander.'

Koenig held up his wrist. 'Morning. Morning for those with a sun waiting to come up. Good morning to you, Paul.'

He stayed a minute, watching the immense, black velvet star map on the big screen and then slowly made his way out. In the corridors, duty personnel changing watch saluted as they passed. All in all, it was still a taut ship.

In his own room, he shrugged out of his tunic and prepared for bed. His own face in a polished steel mirror caught his eye. It was a hard, hawk-like job with lines deepening round the mouth and eyes. He would have to watch it, he was turning into an autocratic bastard.

In Main Mission, Paul Morrow was staring in simple disbelief at the big screen and Sandra Benes, whose delicate fingers had conjured the image from an eteliolated quirk in a wave pattern, said in an awed whisper, 'Holly Cow! Somebody tell me they've seen anything like that!'

An honest man, Kano, looking at it from the computer spread, said 'Not me. Not anywhere,' and was sidetracked by a rapid clatter from his patient friend's outfall. He read it off. Computer was as startled as the next man. 'Computer hasn't either!'

Paul Morrow was already using his intercom. 'Main Mission calling Commander Koenig ... Commander!'

Koenig's face appeared on the miniature screen, 'Paul, this had better be more than urgent ...'

'*It* is right. Commander. This you have to see.'

'I'll be there. Don't let it go away.'

Before Morrow had switched himself out, Koenig was moving for the door, feeling some of his tiredness drop away. A red tell-tale blinked on a bulkhead and alarm klaxons sounded out. Morrow was calling a full team to the operations centre.

Some, with a shorter journey, beat him to it. Others raced in behind him. There was a full crew to watch Sandra get a clear, hard edged picture on the main scanner. Helena Russell, smoothing honey blonde hair off of her forehead; Victor Bergman, balding and grizzled, Alan Carter, chief pilot of the Eagle fleet; all the Main Mission staff stared at the screen.

Tumbling through space, like a tubular nonsense figure, was an object that had no symmetry or regular construction. Its only definite characteristic was that it had motion and the motion was clearly bringing it out of nowhere and into their path.

Koenig said tersely, 'Magnification...'

Seeing it bigger was no bonus. It was still a nothing, but uglier with it.

As the scientific adviser to the outfit, Victor Bergman recognised that he had a duty to define it, but he could only shake his head puzzled. It was left to Kano to begin, 'By all that's scientific, if that's a spacecraft...'

Finding his voice, Bergman said, 'It breaks every known law of aerospace propulsion.'

Koenig said, 'Like the bumble bee, which shouldn't get off the ground by all technical arguments.'

'But it does. True. You have a point there, John. The spoils of ignorance.'

Koenig looked again at the screen, 'Give it the lot, Sandra. Extreme magnification.'

There was a pause, with the screen a jumble of silver rain and then a grainy blow up, which seemed to have collected more stark menace as it bore down on the wandering Moon with a lopsided deliberation. Now, they could identify a section which could be judged as a central core to which were fixed a random collection of long cylindrical projections, each of which ended in a bulbous pod.

Koenig reckoned he was being short changed by his technical advisers. He said harshly, 'Kano. Kick your high speed idiot. Get it to pull its finger out and give us a little information.'

Everybody heard him try. Almost apologetic, Kano said, 'Computer, I want detailed information on the space object.' There was silence. He dropped his sights, anxious for the reputation of his section, 'Anything at all!'

Badgered into speech, the hardware flipped a relay and said coldly, 'I have nothing to say on that subject.'

Kano could hardly meet Koenig's eye, 'Commander, nothing. I don't begin to understand it.'

Helping him out, Computer chipped in again, 'My information is privileged.'

Koenig thumped his forehead with the heel of his hand. It was no time of day to face a mechanical prima donna. As if on cue, a melodious chime reverberated round Main Mission and a new voice joined the group. It seemed to seep out of the very fabric with no source that could be pinpointed. It was mellifluous, educated in timbre and on the whole carried friendly harmonics, like a patronising uncle. 'Good day, dear friends, I would not wish to intrude, but I rather need your immediate help.'

In some ways it was more surprising than a direct challenge or a declaration of hostility. There was uneasiness all round. Sandra Benes, stating the obvious, said, 'We've lost visual, Commander.'

Kano was punching studs all along his spread, 'He's not reaching us by radio waves, Commander . . .'

Confirming it, Morrow said, 'I'm trying all channels. No dice.'

The voice helped them, unctuous and well modulated, 'Not to worry. Our communication is excellent. In a moment, even with your restricted sight, you will see me.'

Clearly, the speaker believed it would be a rare privilege for one and all. Thinking aloud Koenig said, 'Friendly?'

Near enough to catch what was said, Bergman said, 'You'll have to ask louder, John.'

Being on the same personal frequency as Koenig, Helena Russell had also heard the quiet question. There was something about the voice which bothered her. She asked a question of her own. 'Suppose we get the wrong answer?'

Koenig met her eyes, level and serious and answered obliquely, 'Kano. Ask Computer if that thing is armed.'

There was no need, Computer answered for itself, 'I am otherwise occupied.'

They had themselves a joker out of the cosmic hat. A joker, however, with technical knowhow outside their range. Whatever game he wanted to play, he would make the rules for himself. The outlandish spacer was coming in, hovering on the lunar horizon as though waiting to be invited to land. The voice said, 'Do grant permission for me to land on your territory, Commander.'

'For what reason?'

'I need your help. Isn't that reason enough?'

'Possibly.' Koenig looked at Bergman and Helena for their reactions.

Bergman said, 'We are peace loving people. There will be no aggression from this side.'

Thinking of the human side, Helena began, 'What kind of people, do you suppose . . .'

She was interrupted by Alan Carter who was making a gut judgement, 'That thing is hostile.'

'And yet asks for help?' Paul Morrow could not believe that the owner of the voice could do anything except hand round sweets at a Christmas treat.

Carter was not convinced, 'That's just a clever front.'

'Where's your compassion?'

'Survival first, inter-Galactic charity a long way after.'

The stranger had listened to the exchanges. There was no lessening of goodwill as the voice said, 'Far be it from me to hurry your democratic discussions, but I have an emergency.'

It was not nice to know that everything spoken could be overheard and Carter made a stage whisper of, 'And we've got our emergency and *you're* it.'

It earned him a hard look from Morrow and the voice chipped in with, 'Mine is greater than your rather naive fear.'

Nobody liked it. Thoughts themselves might be in question. To make it clear that he was dealing from the top of the deck, Koenig said loudly, 'Very well. You have permission to land.'

There seemed to be no intentional irony in the measured tones, 'I am obliged to you.'

'*Away* from the base.'

'Of course, naturally; one should always be careful with strangers.'

They watched the strange craft hit the surface and trundle itself lightly about, as random as thistle down. Then it picked out a line and was moving directly for Moonbase Alpha. Hostile or not, it was a fascinating thing to watch and Helena was reminded of the morbid interest some could have in watching a spider.

Koenig said sharply, 'Hold it, I gave permission to land not to approach the base.'

The urbane voice was full of reason, 'Can't you see, Commander, that my intentions are pacific?'

'With respect, that is not obvious,' Koenig was falling into the same courtly way of speech.

Still rolling forward, from one ugly pod to another, the device made no effort to stop. Keeping the conversation going, the voice said, 'I only require your assistance.'

Koenig called his Eagle Overlord, 'Alan get two armed Eagles off the deck.'

Speaking to the big screen as a convenient location for the mystery voice, he said, 'They'll fire on my instruction.'

'I must advise you not to do that,' there was a little more steel in the plummy voice.

'And why not?'

'Principally because I won't let you.'

'Go to it, Alan.'

Alan Carter tried. Then he was turning to Bergman and Morrow with complete bewilderment. There was bitterness in his voice as he said, 'Commander, I can't get through.'

The know-all voice was beginning to grate on Koenig's taut nerves. This time, it said evenly, 'Your intercommunication systems will function only when I want them to. Now, Commander, shall we be reasonable?'

The machine had finally come to rest. Maybe honour was satisfied. Koenig said slowly, 'If you come in peace ...'

'If? What is this *if*? My word is my bond.'

Koenig went on, 'Then I'm prepared to receive a small delegation. Unarmed, of course.'

Even as he said it, he knew there would be no agreement. The machine rested a couple of kilometres outside the perimeter. The voice that came from nowhere in particular and used English as though it was an Earth national, put it on the line, 'No, no, Commander. *I* shall welcome a small but distinguished delegation. It will consist of Dr Helena Russell, Professor Victor Bergman and yourself, Commander John Koenig. All *armed*, of course.' The small jest clearly pleased the speaker, but did nothing to reassure the Alphans.

Helena Russell put her hand on Koenig's arm, 'What do you think, John? Are we going?'

'Do we have any choice?'

'A wise decision, Commander. I am delighted. You will not need life support systems.'

When his mind was made up, John Koenig acted swiftly. Leaving Morrow and Carter with a watching brief, he hustled the delegation into a moonbuggy and got under way. Main Mission checked them out, giving a route through protective screens, watching the buggy bounce away over the all too familiar moonscape.

There was silence in the module itself. Bergman was trying to work out how the stranger operated. It was outside rational belief. Whoever had planned it was on a different wavelength from Earth based logic. As they approached, the spidery monster's huge size became apparent. Even the smallest pods at the end of the tubular arms dwarfed the moonbuggy. Helena Russell watched Koenig's hands as he made a neat, competent job of navigating the clumsy craft. Koenig himself had stopped thinking. He would have to play it a step at a time and until he met his adversary, he could do no more.

As they approached, a hatch sliced open in the nearest pod foot and a ramp dropped to the moondust. Koenig stopped, looked at it, then moved forward again. It was altogether too much like a trap, but having come this far, there was no point in being coy. The hatch lifted and shut with a definitive click. He killed the motor and waited.

Helena Russell said suddenly, 'We're moving. Being lifted!'

It was true. A rushing sound had built up. The whole buggy was off the deck and rising through the ceiling of the pod into the tube above. Seen from the inside, the tube was transparent and they could look out over the moonscape to the halls and covered ways of Moonbase Alpha.

Victor Bergman, fairly hopping about with excitement, said, 'Fascinating.'

The voice, beamed to a point in the centre of the buggy, said, 'Don't worry about the mechanics. You're being delivered to my control room.'

In Main Mission, there was anxiety of another sort. As soon as the excursion module had run into the open pod, communication had ceased. There was no joy on any channel. Koenig's party might as well have stepped off the edge of a flat Earth.

A worried man, Paul Morrow said, 'Not a thing. No contact. Nothing.'

Other operators confirmed it, from the communications desk Sandra said, 'No visual.'

Kano was disgusted with his Computer, 'No Computer — again.'

Thumping the Eagle Command Console, Alan Carter came to a decision. 'Right then. I'm taking those Eagles up.'

Morrow was less sure, 'You heard the threat.'

'I heard and that's why I'm following the Commander's original order. We're all being brainwashed by Big Brother out there.'

As if on cue, the plummy voice was at it again. This time, clearly speaking to the visiting team. 'Welcome aboard, Alpha party. Relax and be welcome. Just let yourselves go.'

Maybe it was going for open diplomacy. There was to be communication, but strictly on its own terms. Morrow, Sandra and Kano looked at each other. Alan Carter stood up. If he waited for a decision from them, he would wait a long time. He hurried off for the hatch.

In the interior of the spacer, the moonbuggy had reached journey's end. Doors had opened revealing a landing area and a corridor. Still talking them in, the voice said, 'It's quite safe for you to come out now.'

Koenig thumped his harness release and opened the hatch. They stepped out. Behind them, the elevator doors slid shut and there was a repeat of the vacuum whoosh as the buggy was whipped off to be garaged.

Curious, but cautious, the three Alphans walked slowly along the corridor.

Encouraging them, the voice seemed to speak softly into each head, 'Do come in so that we may be well met.'

Bergman was speaking hardly above a whisper, 'As the spider said to the fly.'

He was taken up immediately, 'Children's stories are brutal, Professor. But you have nothing to fear.'

'Except fear itself.'

'Ah yes. The wise man is he who knows *when* to be afraid.'

Ahead of them, the way was suddenly clear. A vast hemisphere structure opened from the corridor. This was the control room, then? Koenig went in and stopped. The others followed. At their backs, a metal sheet slammed home with a thud and they spun round. The way in was sealed as though it had never existed.

Koenig took a grip on a rising tide of anger and irritation. Actions and words seemed to be on two distinct planes. But they were in and the only course was to go for a meeting with the owner. He said, 'All right. So we look around. When he's finished playing games I suppose we get to meet him.'

There was certainly plenty to see. It was evident that the tumbling motion of the craft was of no importance at the centre. The floor of the half globe would stay level whatever was happening. It was gymbal mounted with some sophisticated, compensatory devices that had Bergman sucking in his breath with admiration.

Switchgear was on a big scale, pedestal mounted and out of reach for a normal human operator. Glowing screens flushed continuously with changing coloured light. The whole interior had been engineered to give the impression of endless space. It was big enough as a physical fact, but subtle colour had been used so that the observing eye was not confronted with a stop. Soft pastel shades suggested immense distances. If the machine had come from nowhere, it carried the same theme at its living centre.

But there were distinct areas at floor level. Gossamer thin screens suggested certain divisions. There was what could be thought of as a 'living' space with chairs and tables. Another which was a 'resting' place with couches. All furniture was of such beautiful construction and such proportion that it seemed to express the quintessence of the function it served.

There was floor space to wander over. Helena touched a chair. It looked like marble, but was light and warm. She was about to speak when an intense beam of light shone down, turning her blonde hair into a pale gold aureole. Then it moved like a free standing column and played around Koenig. From there, it rolled across to Bergman. Except for the startling intensity of the light, there was no discomfort.

For Bergman, the mass of unfamiliar hardware was a delight and a vexation. Mind and body at a stretch, he was trying to make something intelligible out of it. Koenig grinned at Helena and they left him to it. Pushing on into the sleeping place, they continued to search for the host and stopped in their tracks before a couch that was in use. Unbelievably, they had found something to talk to.

It was not what they had expected at all. For a spell, there was silence on both sides. The man stretched out on the bed was so old that Methuselah would have looked like a Spring lamb. Skeleton thin, with a shock of white hair and gnarled, wrinkled hands, he could have been long dead. When the eyelids flicked open and a pair of amazingly bright, searching eyes stared up at them, they stepped back in shock.

Bergman heard Helena's startled exclamation and hurried in. The oldster was moving, jacking himself off the bier with slow deliberate movements.

Once a doctor always a doctor, Helena Russell moved in to help, but the ancient man waved her aside. She had another surprise when the figure spoke. The voice was firm, soft and courteous without any of the harmonics of extreme age.

'I regret not welcoming you on your arrival. I rest only when I must. How can I help you?'

It was nice to have a dialogue with a recognisable hominoid type – even one at the edge of dissolution, but it made no sense. The man waited for an answer. Koenig said slowly, 'It's more a matter of what we can do for you. You summoned us.'

'I summoned you?'

'For help.'

Believing in protocol, Helena Russell thought names might be useful, 'I'm Doctor Russell. This is Commander Koenig – and Professor Bergman.'

The ancient nodded. He made a courtly gesture and walked slowly towards the living space. 'Be seated. I am Companion.'

It was not much in the way of explanation. When they were seated, Koenig tried again. 'Perhaps if you would send for the others they could explain.'

The ancient looked shrewdly at him recognising a hint of condescension. 'I know why you're here, Commander.'

He looked away and addressed empty space, 'You think I don't know what you're doing. Why are you silent, Gwent?'

Koenig looked quickly at Helena. For his money Companion was senile. They would get no sense.

Whether he saw it or not, the ancient went on, 'Gwent? Not speaking? Then I'll speak for you.' The bright eyes focussed suddenly on Helena, 'He's devious. Very devious. Leaves *me* to deal with his lesser chores.'

Bergman asked, 'Where is Gwent?' and was ignored. Companion's voice took a more incisive bite, 'His purpose in coming here is clearly two-fold. I am well aware of the first and can guess the second. But I shall only speak of what I know.'

Making amends, Koenig said respectfully, 'We shall be grateful for any information you can give us, sir.'

'From time to time, we must interrupt our endless journey to obtain certain items necessary to our continued well-being.'

A metallic clatter from a pedestal interrupted. A printout slip was projecting and Koenig reached it half a pace ahead of Bergman.

Suddenly cranky, Companion said, 'So. *Now* you take an interest when you want something. I suppose he's issued a list of his requirements?'

Koenig had skimmed down it and handed it to Bergman. 'Some list. What do you say, Victor?'

'Well, we have most of the basics.'

The voice boomed out with startling volume, 'I've consulted your computer. You have everything I need.'

Companion said, 'Devious, devious. Why have me explain and then interfere?'

'You were handling it badly.'

'Badly? You say *badly*? Then I withdraw. You can tell them whatever you want.'

'You presume too much on our relationship, Companion.'

'I'm glad to hear I can!'

Gwent spoke to Koenig, 'Well now, Commander. Can I count on your co-operation?'

That was a hard one, Koenig knew he had no way of renewing supplies for Alpha. 'We'll do our best. *If* Computer says we can spare all this.'

'I've already told you . . .'

'I'd like to hear that from Computer myself.'

'Very well. Do so. Do so. By all means, do so. Let us proceed through all the proper channels.'

If it was a small victory for Koenig, Companion took the success out of it, 'You're wasting your time, Commander. He controls your Computer. It will say anything he wants it to say.'

Gwent sounded impatient, 'Speak to your Computer. Speak to your staff. Ask your questions. Go on. Do you dispute my word of honour?'

It was not humanly possible to conceal their disbelief. Something of the same feeling was clear in Kano's voice as he tried for the hundredth time to get a reasonable reply from his computer. Punching buttons he said, 'Here we go again, with faith, hope and . . .'

Computer answered pat and might have finished the phrase, 'Gwent's orders have been relayed to Supply Department and await shipment on Dock 4.'

Koenig's voice followed, loud and clear, 'Kano, do you read me?'

'Yes, Commander.'

'I heard that. When was the order given?'

Computer answered for itself, 'Twenty-two fourteen hours.'

In case anybody was having trouble with simple arithmetic, Gwent said, 'Twenty-three minutes ago to be precise.'

'Then *you* presume too much, Gwent.'

Companion relished the reference and his ancient map split in a death's head grin. It took Gwent another five seconds to remember his earlier use of the expression and then a huge bellow of laughter rolled and reverberated around the dome.

'Spoken like a Commander!'

Koenig faced Companion, 'I demand to see Gwent.'

'You do.'

It was softly spoken and Koenig suddenly wheeled round expecting to see the missing joker. Companion went on, 'Everything *is* Gwent.'

It was a new slant and there was a digestive pause as they considered the only meaning.

Koenig said, 'Gwent. This? This machinery?'

It was not popular. Gwent's voice said, 'Machine. Are you calling me a machine!'

'If you're not a machine, show yourself.' There was silence and he turned again to Companion, 'You control this machine?'

'It is true he is not entirely self-sufficient . . . but almost.'

Bergman pressed for a direct answer, 'But you *do* have ultimate control . . . ?'

'Over Gwent? No . . . no. Would that I had . . .'

Gwent's voice had quiet rage in it, 'Control me! Control me!'

Companion raised his voice, 'Some of the time,' – then he lowered it for a quiet aside, 'Seriously, I should do as he says.'

It was so much gobbledegook to Koenig. Either the oldster was in control of the machine or he was not. He tried to force an answer, 'But you *must* control this apparatus.'

There was not much mobility left on Companion's withered mask of flesh. Nevertheless, he contrived to convey a nice blend of laughter at Koenig's naive ignorance and fear of what action his mechanical buddy might take. The struggle to resolve conflicting emotions was taking a toll on his emaciated frame. He did manage to jerk out, 'Oh . . . oh . . . please . . . you must refer to him as Gwent.'

Gwent himself was alarmed at Companion's physical distress. He called sharply, 'Doctor Russell!'

Helena was already on the move. She had been watching Companion and her instinct told her that only a very little was needed to shift him definitively into the land of the dead. Holding him steady, kneeling beside his chair, she said soothingly, 'Don't speak. I can help you.'

She lifted his hand, it was bird frail, the pulse was hardly detectable.

For the first time, there was a ring of genuine feeling in Gwent's voice as he said, 'Companion!' and went on, 'If you're not dead then speak!'

Unbelievably, Companion still could, though the effort was pitiful to see, 'All you care about . . .'

Helena turned to Koenig, 'He's a very sick man.'

Companion was drawing strength from a sheer act of will power, 'I'm fit. These little attacks come and go – mere discomfort.'

'Are you certain, dear friend?'

Companion forced himself to sit erect, too proud to endure pity. 'Don't worry about *my* capabilities. Send for your supplies so that we can be on our way.'

It was meant for Gwent, but Koenig took it as if for himself and Companion went on, 'Quickly. Quickly if you please.'

Koenig said, 'Very well. I'll issue the order the moment we reach base.'

Gwent's voice bellowed 'No! From here.'

'You have *my* word.'

'I believe only in *my* honour. Issue the order!'

Koenig signalled to the others and they followed him to the closed hatch.

Companion had struggled from the chair to make his appeal, 'Please accommodate him in this. He always has his way.'

Gwent said, 'Always.'

Helena looked at Koenig. She hated to see what it was doing

17

to Companion. But Koenig was adamant, 'You'll get those supplies when we get back to Alpha.'

Companion had crossed the floor and was ready to fall. He clutched at Koenig for support, 'No, Commander – no! None of us – not you, not I – can stand up to him.'

'Haven't you *any* influence?'

'Gwent is *my master*.'

He saw their reaction and drove himself on, 'I have always been his companion. I've grown old in his service. I might die, but Gwent goes on forever. He'll let nothing stop him. Forget your human pride. Give him what he wants, then go . . . while you still can.'

The sting in the tail was not lost on Bergman and Helena. It was a clear warning. Helena spoke to the centre of the great room, 'Gwent. Your Companion is close to death. I have no medical equipment with me. If *we* can get him to the medicentre at Alpha . . .'

Pride had once more boosted the dying man. Erect as a spear he walked away from them.

Gwent thundered, 'Enough. Do what I say.'

Koenig's 'No!' – was a matching shout.

'I can blast your puny base from the universe.'

There was a sense of motion though the floor remained horizontal. Watchers in Main Mission saw the machine tumble itself towards Alpha. Koenig flipped open his comlock, 'Paul, immediate launch. Attack to disable.'

Alan Carter answered him, 'Check, Commander. On our way.'

The two Eagles which had been circling at a distance raced in on a bombing dive. Needle thin beams of searing light bored out in concert from the heavy duty lasers. Brilliant asterisks flared on two of Gwent's pod feet as the lines went home. Watchers in Main Mission saw some material sheer and break away, but as the Eagles beat away for a turn it was clear that no vital breach had been made.

In Gwent's control dome, Companion was showing acute distress, but the three Alphans watching the action on the miniature screen of Koenig's comlock saw nothing of it. Gwent himself was wholly concerned with retribution. He said, 'Measure for measure, if that's what you want!'

The Eagles were turning over a jagged mountain feature as Gwent operated some unseen armament. Lights in the globe dimmed and the floor lurched. The whole mountain was bathed in an incandescent glow before it erupted in a vast boiling geyser of atomic trash.

Morrow called urgently, 'Stand by rescue unit,' and Gwent's mocking voice sounded simultaneously in Main Mission and his own control room, 'Truce?'

Koenig knew a demonstration of overkill when he saw one. Grim faced, he called Morrow, 'Cease fire.'

He stared in impotent anger at the iridescent dust cloud where his Eagles had been. At his back Companion suddenly sagged at the knees and crumpled to the deck.

Helena saw the movement in the corner of her eye and ran over, kneeling beside the fallen man. She said urgently, 'Gwent! You must let us go! Your Companion needs medical attention.'

Lights flashed in a spasm round the dome. A column of light built itself and centred on the prone figure.

Gwent said, 'What's wrong with him?' It was brusque, unsympathetic, as though Gwent refused to accept that anything could be allowed to interfere with his arrangements.

Helena made no effort to soften the diagnosis, 'He's dying.'

'Companion must not die.'

'Words alone will not save him.'

Companion's eyes were open. He seemed to appreciate Gwent's concern. But his smile was wry. Sentiment had little place in their long relationship. He said heavily, 'Don't pretend you didn't know I was dying. I said there were two reasons why we came here. I am that second one.'

Accusation in her tone, Helena also addressed Gwent, 'You knew he was dying?'

Gwent was silent. Companion forced himself to speak, 'You don't understand.' Levering himself up on one elbow he went on with something like anger in his voice, 'Tell them you didn't want to admit I was dying. You won't even admit it now will you?'

Gwent's voice was a boom, 'No! You're not dying. You're only feigning – trying to annoy me. Admit it, you old fool.'

A spasm of pain wracked Companion's emaciated body. He just managed to speak, 'I admit nothing... old... *friend*.' His eyes sought Koenig's, 'I'm sorry I leave behind the worst part of me.'

'Gwent?' Part of the riddle was plain to Koenig.

'Yes . . . Gwent is me . . . he took control . . . outgrew his creator. Think of me at my best . . . I have to leave you to his dreadful mercy.'

The ancient body went slack. Not even his fierce pride could hold Companion any longer inside the frail shell. No announcement from Helena was needed to tell the Alphans that their only human link with Gwent was dead.

There was silence under the great dome. Gwent knew the score, but typically refused to accept it. He said, 'Companion?'

Helena Russell stood up, 'Companion is dead.'

Gwent's voice suddenly broke in a savage howl. Lights flared and pulsed and the control room lurched crazily. The probing beam zig-zagged in a mad dance of death around the dome.

'Savages! Blind savages! You've killed him!'

Thrown off their feet, the Alphans clung to the deck as Gwent threw his machine body at random over the moonscape and finally settled for a direct, vengeful drive at Moonbase Alpha.

CHAPTER TWO

Emotion nudged Gwent's unstable personality over the edge of sanity into a manic tantrum of blind temper. Staff in Main Mission were stunned by the sheer volume and demonic power of the shouting voice. 'Rude assassins – stand to attention. Show respect.'

Deranged by grief and remorse, the machine was looking for a scapegoat to unload responsibility which it was not equipped to accept. A burst of pure gobbledegook blared away at immense power and cut short in a sudden silence. The Main Scanner which had whited out on overload came to life again with a view of the moonscape. The machine was tumbling about like a drunk.

Computer, freed from outside control began to work on the backlog of requests. Morrow's intercom net jammed with requests from Alpha sections wanting information.

Security called, 'Security, calling Main Mission, come in please.'

A female operator from Hydroponics began, 'Main Mission. Do you read me . . . ?'

An agitated quartermaster called urgently, 'This is Supply. For godsake can I have instructions for this shipment on Dock Four.'

Making up for lost time, Computer reeled out half a metre of tape from the outfall and Kano had to thump Morrow's back to get his attention. Among the data, there was one item repeated and he reckoned the chief executive ought to know. 'DESTRUCTION OF ALPHA IMMINENT.'

Morrow cleared his board. He tried for Koenig. 'Commander, this is Main Mission. Can you signal?'

Only the computer was still batting. All other operators waited for a reply. None came. Morrow shook his head.

Then, unbelievably, Carter was on the net, his voice crackling with electronic mush. 'Carter here.'

Morrow said, 'Status?'

'Both Eagles damaged but operational.'

An interruption came from Sandra Benes. She had been watching her monitor and threw a picture of the machine to the big screen. 'Look – it's lifting off.'

There was no doubt about it. Tumbling on an erratic flight path that reflected Gwent's demented state, the machine was well above the horizon.

Carter called again, 'I have it in sight.'

'Pursue. Stand by to attack.'

In Gwent's control room, Koenig and Bergman had carried Companion to his couch. Death had brought peace to his time-raddled face. Gwent was keeping an ominous silence and their voices were quiet. The great hemisphere had become a tomb.

Koenig sensed movement, 'We've lifted off.' The complex instrumentation was pulsing with light. Where there had been a slow steady beeping, there was now a thrum of power. He tried to call Main Mission, 'Come in Main Mission. This is Koenig. Do you read me? Come on dammit, answer!'

There was no response and he shoved the comlock back in his belt. Gwent's voice breathed over the quiet room like a curse.

'Savages!'

Needled to reply, Helena Russell said indignantly, 'You can't blame us for Companion's death. If it's anybody's fault, it's *yours*!'

'I will not be accused.'

'But you judge us! I warned you he was ill. I might have saved him.'

There was a pause. When Gwent spoke, he seemed to be trying to be reasonable. 'Yes, so you did. Companion was right. He told me he was dying; but I wouldn't accept that. You see I believe in the power of matter over mind. In the end, Companion proved I was right. But didn't he rage splendidly at the end? If . . . responsibility . . . is a concern that bothers you, I release you from it.'

Dryly, Bergman said, 'Thank you for that.'

It provoked a flash of anger, 'Only Companion is impertinent with me! Now you will prepare him for burial.'

The machine had tumbled itself into space. Carter, driving his battered Eagles, was holding on.

Morrow called, 'Near enough, Alan. Steady as you go. Just stay with it.'

Gwent had pulled another remote controlled trick and extruded a torpedo-shaped casket to the deck. It was clearly custom built for Companion. Koenig slipped catches and took

22

off the lid. Then he carried the frail body and laid it out in the half shell.

Before lifting on the lid, they stood to give tribute to a strange and courageous space farer. Bergman said, 'Companion is ready.'

Gwent's voice was resonant for a funeral ovation. 'I must need speak in passion – but he hears me not . . . Here lies Companion, my first friend . . . who served me without complaint or self-pity. The best of his kind. Gone now. I cherish his memory. His memory . . . remains . . . remains . . . remains.' He seemed to have stuck on a loop and there was a rising note of hysteria.

Playing for time, Koenig took over, 'We commit to eternal space the body of Companion.'

Gwent's voice went emotional, 'Is that all?'

Bergman added, 'Amen.'

Gwent's shriek rang round the dome.

Helena watched the two men as they closed the capsule and snapped down the seals. A circular hatch opened in the dome wall, clearly intended for the launch. They carried it over and slid it forward for a full due. Auto gear fed it along a conveyor and the hatch sliced shut behind it.

Gwent said, 'Matter to matter. Goodbye – old friend.'

The trailing Eagles saw one of the circling pods eject the capsule with tremendous power and it arrowed off into the infinite wastes of the starmap.

Morrow picked up the movement and queried, 'What goes on, Alan?'

Carter was already checking his monitors, 'Sensors indicate . . . you won't like this . . . it's a human body.'

'Live?'

'Dead.'

'Execution of a hostage?'

'Do I close in?'

'No. They'll all be killed. Eagles One and Two return to base. Now!'

He sat staring at his console. Then he moved to a decision and punched a button to bring in Supply. 'Get that load of stores on Dock Four into an Eagle. Be ready to lift off on my order.'

Reluctantly, Alan Carter called off the chase. Turning for

Alpha, he watched the machine dwindling astern. It had been a bad situation from start to finish. Jaw set like a trap, he flung the labouring Eagle on the home course.

Waiting for Gwent's next move, the Alphans in the control dome sat round a table. From the activity level of the panels, it seemed that Gwent had cut outward flight and was holding the craft in limbo. When his voice suddenly sounded out, there was more frantic pulsation as though to speak was to move. The voice itself was back to normal.

'And so dear friends, we have committed Companion to eternity. Thank you for your part. Now we shall return to Alpha . . . I expect you to follow orders. Otherwise I will terminate your lives with all the prejudice at my disposal and do not think for a minute that I make an empty threat.'

To prove the point, three beams seared from the dome and bathed each one of the Alphans, locking them to their chairs. Pain needled them from every cutaneous sense bud. While it lasted, it was torment that could not be imagined. Then it was gone and sick and shaken they clung to the table top.

Gwent said icily, 'A small demonstration.'

Lifting his head, Victor Bergman said, 'We all owe God a death.'

'Good. Good. I admire your spirit, Professor. Old man should rage.'

A dialogue with an adversary which had no human form was difficult. Bergman found he was visualising a head with some of the late Companion's features. He said steadily, 'What would you know of youth or age or the emotions that give a human, biological structure its unique place in the cosmos? You believe that matter and mind are one. But I tell you, Gwent, there is more to being human than that. Companion was greater than you will ever understand.'

Helena said quietly, 'Well said, Victor.' They waited for Gwent to retaliate. But there was silence in the dome. He was concentrating on another task. The machine steadied in flight and settled to a new course.

The big screen in Main Mission saw the change. Steady and determined it was tumbling in the wake of the Eagles towards Moonbase Alpha.

Sandra said, 'It's coming back!'

She was thinking of the hostages and sounded almost pleased. Paul Morrow looked at Kano. For his money, it could be disaster. Kano quoted Computer, 'Destruction of Alpha, imminent.'

Filling Koenig's empty command slot, Morrow had a problem. He could, however, carry through the supply drill. Switching through to the dock, he asked, 'Is Eagle Four loaded with those supplies?'

The pilot himself answered, 'Yes, sir. All ready to lift off.'

'Stand by.'

Gwent's voice was a moody rumble in the control dome of the speeding machine, 'I have no-one to restrain me now. I alone am Gwent.' The voice hardened, 'Commander, give your men the order.'

The vast, unwieldy machine was eating up the distance and boring in for a touch down in the same area that it had used before. Koenig's voice suddenly spoke into Main Mission.

'Paul, can you hear me?'

'Yes, Commander. Loud and clear.'

'We're still alive.'

'All three?'

'Yes.'

Sandra Benes looked blankly round the desks. It did not gell with Carter's report. But there was no time to query it, Koenig was going on, 'Get those supplies ready for shipment.'

'They're all set. Waiting for your instructions, Commander.'

'Thank you. Stand by.'

The machine touched down and rolled jerkily to a stop. Koenig stood in the centre of the floor and addressed Gwent. 'What collateral do I have, Gwent that you will release us once the supplies are delivered?'

The old spirit of sublime self-assurance was back in Gwent's voice, '*Collateral?*'

'Are you going to offer your famous word of honour?'

'Certainly. That will be enough.'

'Not this time it won't.'

A solid column of light materialised and fell like a spear on Koenig. Helena's gasp of dismay chimed with a deep, involuntary groan wrung from the sufferer. Koenig, face set and grim with effort tried to stay erect, but he was beaten down to his knees, pain beating in from every square millimetre of tortured flesh. He was kneeling and then he was pitching forward to the deck with agony whiting out every conscious thought. Lights in the dome dimmed to a red glow, then the pulsating column itself winked out.

Helena was beside Koenig, lifting his head, eyes blind with tears. Gwent's tone of mocking, superiority had never been more offensive when he said, 'You know, Commander, your mindless hostility begins to tire me. Companion's love was a source of strength and joy ... Must I waste valuable energy in punishing you like a child?'

For once he had said too much. Bergman was on it in a flash, 'Waste energy?'

Whether Koenig heard or not, he was committed to a line of action. Gently disengaging Helena's helping hands, he drove himself to sit and then climbed painfully to his feet. When he was erect, he went on as though the interruption was of no importance to the argument, 'Now, Gwent. What about the collateral?'

Gwent sounded too tired to argue, 'Please, no further discussion. When I return, those supplies will be on hand. That is if you have any interest in making the distinction between life and death.'

There was a definitive silence. The lights, which had brightened for Gwent's words, went dim again.

Lowering her voice to a whisper, Helena Russell said, 'Return? What does he mean? Where? Where *from* for that matter?'

Anger was rising in Koenig's head like a red tide. He was sick to death of being at the receiving end of Gwent's megalomaniac tantrums. Challenging, he shouted 'Somewhere, everywhere, where are you, Gwent? There's no point in whispering. Gwent! ... Gwent! Where are you?'

Bergman restrained him. 'John. You can do no good. Now there is something interesting in what he said. He needs to conserve energy. Obviously he's low on vital supplies. That was the prime purpose of this visit.'

Koenig relaxed. It could be the Achilles Heel they were looking for. He said slowly, 'Of course. The lights.'

Helena Russell was stock still, thinking it out. Every organism consumed energy to live. Sooner or later it had to have its particular food. Energy given out had to be replaced. She said, 'Needs. It has needs.'

On another tack, Bergman pointed out an obvious truth, 'Gwent has never lived alone.'

'So it's not only the supplies.'

All three made the next step in the logical chain and the knowledge was as unwelcome as anything yet. They looked at each other as the realisation dawned. Koenig himself put it into words, leaving no area of doubt. 'With Companion dead, Gwent must have a replacement.'

Sitting round a table in the notional recreation area of Gwent's cavernous dome, the three Alphans were each locked in a frustrating mental cycle that brought them back again and again to the same blank wall. Like prisoners through the millennia, they had to come to terms with their helplessness. Gwent had the power and the will to have his way.

In Main Mission also there was a waiting silence. The crazy machine dominated the skyline. Operators sat at their consoles. Only the monitor on Carter's circling Eagle showed movement.

Interior lights in the dome remained low. Koenig suddenly pushed back his chair and stalked to the centre of the floor. He called, 'Gwent! Gwent!'

There was no answer. Gwent was resting his cogs.

Koenig returned to the table and stood behind Helena's chair. She sensed his presence and leaned back her head to touch him. Victor Bergman stood up and walked over to a spread of monitor screens trying to make some sense of the layout.

His sudden gasp of pain broke the silence and Helena beat Koenig by a step to reach him. Grey faced, Victor Bergman was holding his chest, locked in a private world of agony, mouth open in a soundless scream.

Koenig grabbed the tense shoulders as though he could break the bond by external force, but Helena had already read the symptoms. She knew the medical record. 'His heart.'

Bergman's strained eyes gave her the answer. The long strain and Gwent's punitive torture sequence had taken their toll. It was a weakness that had made his appointment to Moonbase Alpha a borderline case and only his own quiet insistence had brought him through the screening procedures.

Koenig carried him, laid him flat. Helena, a doctor without a medical kit or a back up service, began her examination, bitterly aware that she was only going through the motions.

Suddenly, lights in the dome sprang to full power and

Gwent boomed, 'What is your emergency?'

Helena snapped back, 'Heart seizure.' Gwent's probing finger of light flicked round the three Alphans bouncing frantically about as though unable to sort out which was the patient.

Koenig called, 'Will you help us?'

There was a pause with the light still trying to get a clear channel. Gwent sounded uncertain. 'Which of you? Which of you?'

Head on Bergman's chest, Helena Russell said impatiently, 'Are you blind?'

Again there was a pause. Gwent had no wish to admit to any imperfection. Finally he said, 'Separate . . .' There was no move from Helena and the voice was a roar, 'Separate!'

Koenig took her hand and pulled her clear. The light circled and then homed in on the prone figure.

Gwent's diagnosis was instant. 'He had an *artificial* heart. Where he is lying is covered by a force field.'

Helena said, 'The heart's drained of power.'

'Move him.'

Koenig was down in a flash. Lifting Bergman across his arms, he fairly ran with him across the floor to lay him on Companion's empty couch.

There was some relaxation in Bergman's tense limbs and the pain was less severe, but even a layman could see that he was critically ill and under shock.

Koenig said, 'We must be allowed to get him to Alpha for medical treatment.'

'Stand away.'

This time they did. Koenig had his arm round Helena's shoulders, knowing she hated to leave Victor to fight his lonely battle for survival. A crackling beam sizzled through the still air of the dome and focussed unerringly on Bergman's heart.

It was a bizarre, resurrection sequence, a replay of Frankenstein on an updated set. Victor Bergman was in a trauma that seemed likely to shatter his scholarly frame. Gwent said, 'Three thousand volts of electrical energy for five seconds.'

The beam cut. Bergman slumped to the couch. Gwent said triumphantly, 'Done!'

Helena Russell shook off Koenig's restraining arm and ran to the bedside, 'Victor!'

Bergman's face was pale but calm. He could even smile at her anxiety. He patted her hand like a father reassuring a favourite daughter. 'It's all right, Helena. Don't worry. I'm alive . . . and well.'

Proving it by a practical demonstration, he sat up in spite of her attempt to keep him still. When he spoke again, he was close to imitating Companion, 'I am obliged to you, Gwent.'

The reply was testy, 'Oh! You are, are you? . . .'

Koenig caught Bergman's eye and mimed for him to keep the conversation going. Meantime, he crossed to the table and began to write in large letters on the surface with a chinagraph marker from his belt pouch.

'Of course. Surely you understand gratitude?'

'You ask questions like Companion. I miss him. We understood each other . . . in spite of petty differences. He was such marvellous company.'

'Were you actually friends?'

'Companion and I were fellow seekers . . . travelling together forever through the universe. Or so we thought.'

'Everything changes. That is the great truth. Change is the only reality.'

'Except me. I don't change. Companion always relied on me.'

Koenig had finished his message and tipped the table for them to read. 'I THINK HE'S BLIND.'

Bergman went on blandly, 'But also you always relied on Companion.'

Except for a dubious 'Mmm,' Gwent made no reaction. Still at the table, Koenig switched his comlock to visual and brought in Main Mission.

Morrow and his staff got the picture on the big screen. There was no mistaking the mime. Finger on his lips, Koenig was asking for utter hush.

Morrow lifted his hand to signal agreement. Only the hum from the consoles and the occasional rattle from Computer could be heard. Still aloft, Carter was circling endlessly in his patrolling Eagle.

Koenig wrote across the table, 'PREPARE.' Main Mission went tense waiting for the payoff.

Blind, Gwent might be, but his intuition about anything going on in his dome was uncanny. He said coldly, 'Commander, since you are using that device to communicate with your subordinates, order your men to deliver my supplies. Now!'

The three Alphans braced themselves for some punishing stroke. None came. Morrow and Main Mission staff looked their disappointment, shared by Carter who was thumping his console with a balled fist.

Koenig was going on. He was judging that Gwent had the basic idea that communication was taking place, but still had no exact notion of what was being said. He wiped clear his first message and began again. 'A . . . T . . .' He paused conscious that sweat was standing out on his brow. Still writing, he spoke to Gwent.

'Gwent, I've given you a lot of thought.'

'So you should.'

'You are not getting those supplies. It's you or us.'

The word was done. The big screen in Main Mission had it in banner headline A-T-T-A-C-K.

Morrow slammed round his console. Red alerts blinked from every communications post in Moonbase Alpha and strident klaxons sounded out. Armed Eagles, held ready in their hangars, rolled out for launch. It was total mobilisation and Main Mission staff leaped into top gear. After all the frustration, it was almost welcome. At last, they felt they were taking the initiative and that there was some hope of a break out of the deadlock.

Carter picked up a squadron of Eagles and led them in for a strike. In the interval, he had made up his plan. He thought it was probable that the central structure held the Alphan hostages. Avoiding that, he designated targets and his Eagles peeled off and strafed selected pods.

On the ground, Morrow had run out a column of armoured buggies on remote control. As they raced for Gwent over the stark moonscape, Carter found time to shout, 'Good thinking, Paul. Nice to have ground support!'

Morrow said grimly, 'You're welcome.' His big screen was an animated battle map and he had his hands full.

Koenig had a spectator's view of it on the miniature screen of his comlock. The shuddering of the control dome chimed with Eagles' strikes. Ominously calm, Gwent said, 'So. You think it is better to negotiate from strength – puny as it may be.'

Koenig said, 'Not negotiating, Gwent. That is *your* word.'

The dome lurched. Needled into action, Gwent had made a response. He fired again and again. Each time the interior lights dimmed to a glow. He was concentrating on the land force and at each savage burst, one of the racing moon buggies was irradiated in a bright asterisk of intense, cadmium yellow flame. As the flame died it was gone, dispersed as molecular trash.

Bergman looked at the dimming lights and then at Koenig. Could they hope that Gwent would finally exhaust his reserves of power?

Gwent paused long enough to say 'Do I understand you aright, is this a moral issue?'

Koenig, holding on to a table as the floor rocked again, said, 'That's about it, Gwent. It's a matter of intelligent sacrifice.'

'Intelligent? What kind of intelligence is there in that? Are you quite mad?'

He was working systematically along the line of mooncraft and Helena had to struggle to keep on her feet as she said, 'You are nothing but a pirate, a marauder, a kidnapper, looting and pillaging the universe.'

A tremendous burst of energy from Gwent's armament engulfed a whole group of buggies and opened up a brand new crater on the Moon's ravaged map. Gwent shouted, 'Are you counting the cost, Commander?'

'I believe so. To both of us!'

Gwent turned his fire to the Eagles. A searing rope of fire from one of the pods snaked out and homed on the underbelly of a turning craft. The pilot's voice came through laced with static, 'Rescue unit! Area twelve.'

The Eagle was down in a cloud of moondust.

'Still counting the cost, Commander?'

There was a sneer in it and Bergman said simply, 'We're willing to risk our lives to stop you.'

Carter's Eagles were in for a concerted strike and the battery shifted the machine and rolled it a half kilometre. Gwent's growl had a sombre finality in it, 'You have chosen. So be it.'

The machine stabilised itself. One of the pods, jutting into the moon sky, swung and aimed for the sprawling complex of Moonbase Alpha. A bolt of energy crackled out over the ancient rocks and an intense glow surrounded Main Mission like a golden aureole.

Swiftly, every interior and exterior surface began to heat. They were to be fried alive. It was unendurable. The light deepened to a cherry red. Eleliolated screams came from the comlock in Koenig's hand. He had condemned his people to an agonising death. Paul Morrow's voice was just audible, 'Commander . . . help!'

Koenig hunched his shoulders. It was defeat and he knew it. Whatever happened to Gwent, he could not let them take it. He said, 'Hold your hand, Gwent. We will do whatever you say.'

There was silence. Gwent was savouring it. Another Eagle caught in crossfire from two pods screamed down in a death dive. Koenig, blind with anger shouted, 'What words do you want, Gwent?'

'Surrender is sufficient.'

Koenig called, 'Commander to Moonbase, cease fire. Recall all Eagles!'

The glow died around Main Mission. Thickly, Paul Morrow called off the attack. 'Cease fire. Come in, Alan.'

Carter was still circling, debating whether or not to go it alone and Morrow said again, 'Alan, come in. This means you.'

'Understood.' Carter circled once more and dived for his launch pad.

Main Mission came back to normality. All knew they had skirted the edge of the diamond moment of death. Gwent's voice, assured and urbane again, was an insult, 'So much better to see reason – dear friends.'

He went on to speak to his three internees, 'You must believe me. I admire your spirit. Now these are my terms. Professor Bergman. Because of your age and defective condition, you will return to base in exchange for my supplies.'

Victor Bergman looked angrily about him. To be judged and found wanting by a machine was too much. Before he could speak, however, Gwent was at it again, 'Commander Koenig and Doctor Russell must stay with me as my Companions, for as long as you both shall live. I sense there is already a bond between you. In time our relationship could be agreeable.'

Helena's horrified 'No!' interrupted him. The prospect of imprisonment with Koenig was not the issue. This would be a shotgun contract and a life together in the presence of a blind fiddler. Koenig tried to comfort her, holding her close.

Bergman made a bid of his own. 'No, Gwent. You need a man of science to understand your ways. Keep me. I'm in better condition than you think. Don't you understand that with this artificial pump, I have a better life expectancy than my colleagues. Just help me from time to time and I shall be your Companion for many years to come. I know something about loneliness. We shall do well together.'

Helena freed herself from Koenig, 'Victor. You are the best and dearest friend.'

'It's for the best, Helena. Don't you see? Far better me than you and John.'

Koenig said shortly, 'Better no one.'

Still trying, Victor Bergman said, 'It *has* to be me, John. Can *you* promise to live beyond tomorrow?'

Gwent was tired of the argument, 'Promises! I decide who stays, who goes, who lives, who dies. The Professor goes. Get those supplies.'

His voice had hardened. He was ready to demonstrate again where the final power lay.

Bitterly, Koenig spoke into his comlock. 'Prepare to lift off supplies.'

Paul Morrow answered, 'Check, Commander!'

It was clear enough that Main Mission accepted there was no more they could do. Koenig snapped his comlock shut and shoved it in his belt. He had wanted a homecoming with Helena for long enough. But not like this. His hundred million planets had shrunk to a little room in the maw of a mechanical maniac. He could not meet Helena's eyes.

Alan Carter set it up to take any chance that might come his way. Tough skinned as Gwent undoubtedly was, there might just be less armour on the inside. He took three security guards to ride shotgun on the supply waggon and saw they were armed with the heaviest calibre lasers that could be hand fired.

Watching the party on his monitor, Paul Morrow could see the look on Carter's face. If there was any way of getting to the hostages, Alan Carter would be there.

The war party hurried along the corridor from Security and piled into a travel tube for Dock Four. When he picked them up again, they were pounding up the ship hatchway tube into the waiting Eagle. Two supply details were at the hatch and the boxes of supplies were already stacked inside. Carter mimed for them to leave and say nothing. He was playing the sequence in silence. Gwent's perambulating ear would have nothing to report.

Last aboard, Carter lifted his thumb. Morrow breathed, 'And the best of luck go with you.'

Eagle Four jacked herself off the pad in a flurry of moondust, dropped to a metre above ground level and arrowed away like a surface craft for the monstrous machine on the horizon.

When she was still a kilometre off, one of Gwent's grounded pods flipped open a huge hatch and extruded a boarding ramp. Carter lined up his ship, set her down with mathematical accuracy and drove forward out of an instant grey cloud. The Eagle crawled up the ramp like an angular slug and was gone. The ramp retracted. The hatch closed.

Gwent announced it to the only person who had any proper interest in a relief column, 'Professor Bergman, you'll be delighted to know the Eagle has arrived. Your incarceration is nearing an end.'

Helena and Koenig tried to make it easy for him. Forcing some kind of resigned cheerfulness, they stood either side of him to lead him to the hatch.

Bergman was not deceived. He tried one more time, 'Gwent, let them go.'

'No. You weary me, Professor.'

Koenig found the will to say it, but could not look at her as he did so, 'At least let Dr Russell go. You only need one. Let that be me.'

'Deprived of *your* companion, you would be a sullen and moody traveller. No!'

Eagle Four had been lifted and shunted around until it was positioned to offload into the main corridor leading to Gwent's control dome. Carter was stalking about facing the great sealed hatch with his massive laser held two handed. Behind him, his security men dumped the cases in piles and then joined him, each carrying a similar weapon. When they were lined up in front of the door, he announced himself, finding it difficult to talk to an unseen host. 'We have all your supplies . . . Sir. Everything on your list. Where do you want them?'

Gwent's voice was from everywhere and nowhere, 'You have brought everything?'

'All accounted for . . . Sir.'

'I'll make my own check.'

From overhead a probing finger of light materialised and

began to roam around the piles of cases.

The four Alphans were stock still watching the door, waiting. Suddenly the finger of light shifted over and centred on Carter himself. He flinched. The light ran along the barrel of the laser, stopped, repeated the sequence. Gwent's laugh had no element of jollity in it, 'Ah, ah ah! Do I detect a weapon?'

On the other side of the door the hostages exchanged glances. They heard Carter's inspired lie, 'No, Sir. That's a comlock. Part of our communications system. We all carry them.'

The light shifted again, taking each man in turn. It was an eerie investigation. Although there was nothing specific to feel, each one felt that the probe was missing nothing even down to the thoughts in his head.

Gwent was sarcastic, 'Indeed you do. All four of you.' He sighed, 'Ah me. It's no good trusting humans. Always trying out your mindless schemes. Do you take me for a fool? Get out of here with your child's toys!'

Carter stood his ground, 'But the Professor . . . You promised to release the Professor.'

Gwent's voice boomed and reverberated, 'That was before your treachery. Out, Out! The Professor stays with me. Get out!'

Angrily, Koenig said, 'You're not letting him go?'

'No! Tell your men to return to their craft, before I do something you'll regret.'

Koenig hated to put Helena in jeopardy again, but he knew he had no choice. Drawing his laser, he flicked the stud to destructor beam and called, 'Alan, do you read me?'

'Check, Commander.'

'Concerted fire at the door. Now!'

Four heavy duty lasers fired as one. The great blank barrier was irradiated with asterisks of searing light. From inside Bergman and Helena joined the barrage, then seeing they were making no impression, wheeled away and fired at random into the banks of instrumentation. Blasting around, they should have reduced the interior to a smoking ruin. Gwent's metallic bowels were unmarked. One by one, they stopped firing.

Outside, Carter had called a halt. The whole party looked stupidly at the undamaged door.

Gwent's long gale of laughter was the last, contemptuous insult.

He said, coldly, 'Pitiful! What a pitiful performance. You're only good for killing each other.' He laughed again and then cut short for a demonstration of his own power. Pulsating beams dropped precisely to centre on each Alphan inside and outside the control chamber. One by one they were beaten to their knees and then to the floor as the agony broke their hold on their personal worlds of resolution and human dignity.

Even when the beams died, they still lay on the deck afraid to move.

Gwent had no further interest. He was concerned with his own comfort. Ironically, he said, 'Gwent giveth and Gwent taketh away. Now, Professor. You are to join us. Perhaps, indeed, I shall find some small use for your limited knowledge and experience.'

Gingerly, Carter's men were slowly getting to their feet, waiting for Gwent to strike again. Instead they had a contemptuous dismissal, 'Be thankful I am letting you go. Take your primitive machine and get out before I change my mind and kill you.'

They moved slowly into the Eagle. Last to leave, Alan Carter looked dejectedly round the area. He had never felt more helpless. But in truth there was nothing else to be done. The elevator hatch snapped shut. The Eagle began its descent to the entry port.

Main Mission saw the distant pod open and the Eagle was literally thrown out, skidding and slewing in moondust before Carter gained control and lifted it off in a course for Moonbase Alpha. There was gloom all round the desks. Typically Gwent rubbed their noses in it, '*You* are defenceless against me. No more demonstrations!'

There was a time of silence and apathy in the dome. They had lost. Defeat hung heavily in the air. Each one was trying to adjust to a bleak future. Gwent's voice was heavy with a kind of human fatigue, 'And now my dear . . . Companions. You will open those supplies.'

The great door sliced away. A probing finger of light moved slowly over the cases and came to rest on one. 'That one is the first.'

Between them, Koenig and Bergman hefted the crate and carried it inside. The door slammed shut at their backs. Another pencil of light made a pointer, indicating a slot which had opened in the dome wall.

'Unpack the crate.'

Koenig shoved away snap catches and lifted the lid. It was fuel, made up to Gwent's specification in metre-long rods.

'Take out a rod. Insert it where you see the feed port.'

Koenig balanced a rod across his palms and looked at Bergman. Then he said simply, 'No.' Bergman's 'No' followed in the same tone.

The pointing finger glowed more intensely. 'Do you imagine that passive resistance can serve against me?'

Punishment rays struck from the height of the dome. Either he was building a tolerance to it or Gwent was lower on power, but Koenig found he could still keep on his feet.

Gwent's voice was tired, 'When will you learn to obey? Do you have to die?'

Recovery was faster for Koenig, he said, 'Perhaps. But then, are you immortal? I think you are tiring, Gwent. You didn't hurt us so much this time.'

Anger revived the machine's flagging energies. There was something of the old boom, 'I have enough power to destroy you three and your entire base. For the last time, I warn you!'

Bergman yawned, 'Oh come on: get it over with.'

Helena joined in, 'Yes, use up your precious power. Kill us all. Then who will take care of you? You haven't the strength to go elsewhere and find other *Companions*. You're terminal, Gwent! We're your last hope of survival.'

Gwent's voice was a hoarse rasp, 'There's no truth in what you say. I demand . . . your . . . co-operation.'

It was the first crack in the dyke. Koenig felt that the initiative was moving his way. He knew he must keep Gwent alert and talking. 'Our co-operation? Why? We don't know who you are, where you come from or where you're going.'

Pride needled Gwent. There was an excess of vigour to his boast, '*I* am Delmer Powys Plebus Gwent of the planet Zemo. I was a man of the first importance on that planet. Perhaps not recognised as the scientific genius I am. This machine is an extension of myself. I programmed my entire personality into it by a computer language of my own invention. My affective and cognitive aspects are fused with the immense range of a computer's brain and the might and power of a machine impervious to destruction. I have power to destroy a whole planet. That is who and what I am. Delmer Powys Plebus Gwent!'

Koenig picked up a fuel rod and held it above his head, 'Well

Delmer Powys Plebus Gwent, you have won some battles, but now you lose the campaign.'

Gwent sensed the action to come, 'Don't . . . Please!'

'Use your last energies in a paranoid's frenzy. Destroy us, if you wish. In the end, you die.' He smashed the rod across the open crate and fragments skidded away over the floor.

There was an element of pleading in Gwent's tired tones, 'I misjudged you. My experience . . . over all these years . . . travelling the universe alone . . . blind . . . dependent on Companion, has left me untrusting . . . suspicious. Cynical; perhaps, indeed, paranoid.'

There was enough pathos in it to move Helena. She said gently, 'I'm very sorry.'

The tone had gone low key. Gwent had climbed down from his Olympian heights to a human stature. There was even emotional stress. 'You see, having built this machine to preserve my personality, too late I discovered its inherent flaw. I need *company*. None of us exists except in relation to others. Alone, we cease to have identity. Isolation is annihilation. Do you understand?'

They did and they were moved by it. This was Companion speaking. But Koenig realised they must think first of their own survival.

Bergman said, 'You were on the wrong tack from the beginning, dear Gwent. To wish to preserve oneself is the ultimate vanity.'

'Yes . . . yes . . . you are right. It was vanity. The first and last of all the sins that flesh is heir to. I come to welcome my release; thank you.'

His voice was failing. Lights in the dome were going out one by one. Suddenly, Helena called out, 'The oxygen is going . . .'

Koenig rushed for the door and hurled himself against it. There was no joy. It was locked tight. Back against the smooth surface he shouted, 'Gwent! The door. Open the door. Let us out!'

There was no answer. Bitterly, Koenig said, 'We've been too successful. He's killed himself . . . and us with him.'

Breathing was a chore. They sat at a marble table hardly able to believe that success and defeat had been so close.

Koenig opened his comlock and Morrow's voice called urgently, 'Commander. What's happening in there?'

Tight lipped, Koenig said, 'Gwent's dead. We're trapped in here.'

From Morrow's angle it looked like hope, 'I've sent an Eagle out.'

'No good, Paul. You can't get in.'

Bergman slowly fell forward over the table top. Helena Russell tried to reach him and the effort shoved her oxygen starved brain over the edge. She was out, arms outstretched, hair spread in a fan.

Koenig set his comlock on the table and dropped to the deck on all fours. Crawling painfully, he collected a fragment of fuel rod and drove himself to reach the charging port. Clumsily, he shoved the scrap into the hole and leaned his forehead on the wall. His voice was a croak, 'Gwent . . . save us . . .'

No voice replied, but a scatter of overhead lights strengthened. Koenig saw them in double vision. He said, 'No . . . oxygen . . . oxygen. Door . . . open . . . door . . .'

From somewhere there was a subdued hiss and Koenig gasped convulsively as the gas reached his labouring lungs. At a staggering, weaving run, he crossed the floor to reach Helena.

He heard and did not hear a rush of feet at his back. The great door had lifted a metre and Carter was in with his security team. Koenig lifted Helena himself and with Carter beside him carried her to the hatch. Hands lifted her through. Lights were going out one by one. The great chamber was almost entirely dark. Outside, a single light lit the corridor and outlined Koenig as a sharp silhouette. Gwent said, 'Goodbye, dear friends.'

Main Mission put on a ticker tape welcome. Soberly, Koenig turned from the bright friendly faces and went to the observation platform. Morrow followed anxiously, 'Sure you're all right, Commander?'

'I'm fine.'

On the horizon, the gaunt figure of Gwent was still holding station. Sandra Benes checking monitors said urgently, 'It's moving. It's still alive.'

Laboriously, lurching from pod to pod, the machine was under way, tumbling towards Moonbase Alpha. Staff left their desks to see it in clear through direct vision ports. Alan Carter said, 'It's coming right towards us!'

They saw it gain a few metres of height, then touch down and rise again. The bounce that took it over the roof of Main Mission cleared the fabric by less than half a metre.

Koenig said, 'Sandra! Get him on visual.'

The big screen gave Gwent the full treatment as he strode erratically over the moonscape, trying and failing to gain sea room. Dead ahead, a low range of hills came into the shot.

Kano said, 'It's not lifting.'

Gwent rolled on. Koenig was willing him to lift and get clear and end as he had begun in the wastes of the outback which he had made his own. But the mooncliffs loomed ahead like a wall. Gwent seemed to accelerate and rush to his destruction. Then the screen whited out and a second later the foundations of Main Mission picked up the shock wave in a tremor that knocked personnel off their feet.

When the screen cleared, Gwent was gone. Dust and rubble marked the spot. They felt the pity and the waste of it. He had been a seeker as they were themselves.

Koenig walked slowly to his command office. Helena Russell had seen his face and knew the mood. She found him sitting at his desk, head in his hands. More to himself than to her, he said, 'A lonely, blind, thinking creature looking for his death.'

She pulled up a chair and sat facing him across the desk. A good MO's task was never done. Clearly she had a case for treatment.

CHAPTER THREE

Victor Bergman reckoned that even Gwent might have shown some interest in the set up of the experimental lab which he had made his own in the Technical Section of Moonbase Alpha. The remnants of many projects were littered around. Some had been practical matters, designed to solve problems that had come up as time made it necessary to find alternatives to keep the base viable without shipments from workshops on Planet Earth. Some looked ahead, recognising that Science had a duty to seek for advances; even if there was no immediate application.

One success had been a reclaim process for polyurethane foam. He had devised a sealed system where the scrap was heated to 400 Celsius with a water additive. After distillation the residue was a factory fresh product which could be re-used by Maintenance for the many repair jobs needed to stop the base turning to a high grade slum.

His pride and joy was a small prototype engine. If and when the Alphans made a landfall, he wanted them starting as high or higher on the technological scale as the civilisation they had left.

Koenig found the lab a surefire cure for pessimism. It chimed with his own thinking. His worst nightmare was one where he and his staff slowly regressed until they were eking out a savage, subsistence economy in the sprawling base, without the will or discipline to keep themselves ahead.

Bergman, hunched over a work bench was glad of a break. 'Problems, John. Problems. But I believe I have it licked.'

'What's this one, then?'

'Conventional engines are notoriously inefficient. Anything using heat. Hardly ever better than forty percent effective, sometimes as low as ten.'

'Eagle motors?'

'Right. I don't say we can manufacture anything on that scale yet. But sometime, who knows?'

Koenig knew the signs. 'You want to tell me and I want to listen. Go ahead.'

'The question I ask myself is why can't we turn chemical

energy directly into movement as a muscle does?'

'What answer do you give yourself?'

'It's a matter of the mode of combustion. I want to impart a directional velocity to the molecules instead of the random turbulence of thermal agitation.'

'A lot of people have wanted to do that.'

'I've had some help from our chemists. They've managed to grow some splendid TNT crystals. Absolutely regular. No thermal disorder. Now I've tried cooling them to near absolute zero in a vacuum and detonating them. What do I find?'

'Tell me.'

'A parallel beam of fast *cold* particles. A turbine in that stream would convert better than ninety per cent of the explosive force.'

'It sounds good.'

'It *is* good John. Think of it! A completely cold, super efficient propulsion unit. The applications would be endless. For instance . . .'

His example was never given. The communications post flipped a red tell-tale and Koenig spoke into the communicator. 'Commander.'

Paul Morrow's face appeared on the screen. 'We have a signal, Commander.'

'Source?'

'Sandra's working on it.'

'I'll be there.'

Bergman had left his bench and was beside him. They exchanged sober glances. Experience told them it could be bad or it could be good. Koenig said, 'There has to be somebody else out there. Maybe it's a customer for your engine.'

Main Mission was pulsing with suppressed excitement. The big screen was holding the picture of a spacer still far distant, but clearly of great size. It was a conglomerate, never launched from the gravity well of a planet surface, but obviously built in space for an interstellar odyssey. Repeaters were throwing up the drone of a repeated electronic signal.

Helena Russell joined Koenig and Bergman, eyes shining as she looked up at the scanner. 'What do you think, John?'

'I'd say it was a huge transporter. Not a military craft. But that's not to say it doesn't carry armament.'

Bergman had been using grid references and making rapid calculations. His voice was flat with disbelief, 'Fifty kilometres long. Two kilometres diameter. What kind of transporter is that?'

Koenig said, 'A hundred square kilometres. It's a city state!'

Computer clattered urgently and extruded a print-out. Kano tore it from the outfall and swivelled on his chair to face Koenig.

'I have a decode.'

'Let's hear it.'

Kano punched a line of buttons and Computer sorted the data for verbal delivery. The calm voice was at odds with the content, 'EMERGENCY. EMERGENCY. THIS IS THE COMMANDER OF THE SPACESHIP DARIA . . .'

There was a mixed response round the listening circle. Maybe it was not a passing liner able to pick up drifters from a raft, but a fellow derelict. The ongoing signal confirmed it. 'A MAJOR CATASTROPHE HAS OCCURRED. LARGE AREAS OF OUR SHIP ARE DEVASTATED. THOUSANDS OF OUR PEOPLE ARE DEAD. HUNDREDS SICK AND DYING. WE WHO SURVIVE WILL PERISH WITHOUT URGENT MEDICAL AND MATERIAL AID. PLEASE HELP US. OUR LIFE TYPE CONFORMS TO 45OX 294H . . . EMERGENCY. EMERGENCY. THIS IS THE COMMANDER OF SPACESHIP DARIA.'

The Mayday call was on a loop. Kano cut it. The tireless pulsing electronic signal took over on the repeaters. It fell into a pool of silence. The situation was too near home for comfort. Every member of Main Mission staff could imagine their hurrying Moon platform probing ever deeper into the outback of space with a similar signal going out from the transmitters.

A bleeper on Morrow's command console had him checking new data. He said, 'We're picking up life signs, Commander.'

Koenig leaned over Sandra's shoulder and helped himself to the magnification toggle. On the big screen, there was a rush of silver rain and the alien ship reformed in close-up.

The distant monster ship was turning with a slow roll that brought all its structural features into vision. Alan Carter said, 'It may not be too late, Commander.'

If Koenig heard, he did not answer. He was staring intently at the superstructure of the lumbering giant. It was answering no questions. Set on the black velvet pad of the starmap like a gleaming jewel, it was intact and functional. Whatever crisis triggered the continuing signal, it was internal. The bland face of the spacer concealed all. For that matter, it would have to be so. Any torn, gaping holes in the shell would mean destruction and no intelligent life left to ask for aid.

Helena Russell asked quietly, 'What do you think?'

Koenig straightened up. He had come to a decision. They had a duty as spacefarers. If they were ever to expect help, they had to be prepared to give it. He said, 'It's a team mission. I'd like you along, Paul, to make assessment of material damage; Victor, scientific advice; Helena, medical judgement. One security man for this preliminary trip. Lowry in that slot. Alan, have Eagle One brought up for immediate launch.'

Carter's 'Check, Commander,' showed he was pleased to have a change. Before anybody could raise a counter argument, he was striding away for the hatch.

Koenig went on, 'Tanya, Sandra, keep all communication frequencies wide open . . . any response from that ship, relay it through to Eagle One.'

There was no doubt that, with Paul Morrow on the expedition, Sandra would not miss any relevant blip. Her, 'Check, Commander,' was instantaneous.

Flanked by Helena and Victor Bergman, Koenig made for the hatch. At the foot of the small flight of stairs that led out of the operations well, he paused and turned round, 'Kano . . .'

'Commander?'

'Take charge of the shop. Don't sell unless you get a good offer.'

Main Mission settled for a watching brief. Kano sat thoughtfully at his Computer console, leaving the command desk empty. Sandra Benes tuned for a distant view of the great spacer so that she could follow Eagle One from its launch pad. Signal noise continued as a backdrop. There was no change in the message. When Kano hit a button to have it in clear, Computer said, '. . . DEAD HUNDREDS SICK AND DYING WE WHO SURVIVE . . .' He cut back to the pulse note. There was nothing fresh.

Sandra looked across at him. The same thought was in both their minds. There was no telling how long that signal had been blasting out into the interstellar wastes. It could be decades, centuries even. The situation might have changed. The ship could be a vast wandering hulk peopled by the dead, a necropolis of the space lanes.

Kano said, 'The Commander knows what he's doing. They'll be all right.'

Eagle One was clawing out into the starmap. Onboard computers relayed course data. There was work for all hands. Sandra relaxed. A ship meant people. New faces. After their long lonely stint it would be wonderful to talk with other travellers. She concentrated on a refined tracking ploy that brought the distant craft closer as Eagle One ate up the space between them.

Koenig leaned forward against his harness as though by moving a few centimetres he could see through the blank hectares of cladding and unravel the mystery. Eagle One flew in, turned and ran the length of the spacer. The central structure was an immense cylinder which had clearly been assembled from ring sections. Subsidiary cylinders had been clewed on, bulking out the huge body. An elliptical dome area was lit more brightly than the rest. At intervals along either side stubby tubular members of some transparent material ended in mammoth torpedo shaped structures with blank, seemingly solid walls. Eagle One was scaled down to the size of a gnat roaming over a buffalo.

In the passenger module Helena, Bergman, Lowry and Paul Morrow watched from direct vision ports. The pile of medical and rescue equipment in the freight bay seemed suddenly a nonsense. If there was trouble aboard the monster it would need the resources of a major city to sort it out.

Seen close, there was an air of quiet menace about the craft. It was a modern *Marie Céleste* on a mind bending scale.

Carter said flatly, 'No sign of a way in, Commander.'

'Do another circuit, Alan.'

Carter's face showed he doubted the wisdom. They had done their Samaritan bit by answering the signal, if nobody wanted to know, he reckoned they could get back to Moonbase Alpha and watch the derelict drift off.

He turned slowly and ran in again, taking Eagle One a steady hundred metres from the starboard flank of Leviathan. They passed one of the huge, blank pods and then another. At the third there was a change and Helena's startled gasp from the passenger module came up on the intercom.

The pod changed colour. From dull gun metal it glowed silver and then white. Helena's exclamation chimed with Carter's sudden burst of activity. Eagle One was shuddering along its axis and losing way.

Listeners in Main Mission heard Carter say, 'Holy Cow. There's no power. The motor's gone dead.'

Koenig was checking the co-pilot spread. Dials had zeroed, but there was no damage report from the trouble shooter. 'It's a controlled shutdown.'

'We've activated some kind of auto docking system.'

Bergman called through, 'Can you override it?'

At the same time there was new data from the pod. Helena said, 'It's opening!'

Eagle One had stopped all forward motion. Slowly and firmly, she was shifting sideways to the open port. Carter said, 'No dice, we're being drawn inside. All Eagle Systems are smothered.'

Koenig snapped, 'Break it, Alan.'

Carter tried. Using every trick in the manual, he worked at it to get a little life from his dead motors. He ended thumping his console with a balled fist. 'Nothing. No use.'

Eagle One was on the threshold of a monumental hangar. Koenig hit a switch to bring in Main Mission. His monitor screen was bright with silver rain. He called, 'Eagle One to Main Mission. Do you read me?'

There was no answer.

Kano was calling on his own account, 'Come in Eagle One. Do you read me? Come in Eagle One.' Hardly daring to look at Sandra, he watched the tiny Eagle slip inside the open port. Behind it, the great hatch slowly closed.

Inside the pod there was an eerie half light but enough to see that the whole Eagle fleet could have been docked. It was enough to see also that the internal structures were in disrepair. Overhead gantries were sagging. Cladding plates were peeling off and some had fallen neglected in random heaps on the deck.

Dotted around the walls, square features protruded into the hangar and Eagle One was slowly edged along until its main hatch was aligned to one. A tube extruded itself and clamped to the Eagle's hatch coamings.

Bergman said, 'An airlock system.'

Koenig was still trying for communication. 'Emergency signal, Alan. Broad spectrum.'

There was a stifled, whining noise from the gear. Carter said, disgustedly, 'It's a wash out! Jammed solid!'

'Try internal. See if we can contact any of the people on this ship.'

In the rumble, the supercargo were shrugging out of harness and moving about. Alan Carter was slamming round his console still trying to get a little joy. 'It's no good, Commander.'

Koenig tried his comlock. The small screen was streaked with white lines. Its only contribution was a savage burst of static. He replaced it in his belt and watched Carter work one more time round his control panel. Stabbing the release clip of his harness he said, 'Well. We came on a goodwill mission. We've arrived. The question is can we get out again?'

There was no answer from the gaunt dilapidated cavern of a hangar. The Eagle was isolated in a silent junk yard. Carter finally gave up. There was nothing he could do. He said, 'The beam's a one way ticket, Commander. We're trapped.'

Koenig saw his own hawk face on the windshield and looked through it to the desolation outside. If it was true that they were trapped, it was a poor way to go. They would be condemned by their own ethical code. They had answered a distress call in good faith. There had to be more to it than lingering death by starvation on a derelict.

Victor Bergman rummaged in the freight bay and brought out some of the diagnostic gear he had assembled. It was always amazing to watch him in action. Seemingly clumsy, his hands moved over the equipment with a sure, delicate touch. He had assumed there might be problems and had worked out a screening system for a sampling unit and a small, compact computer.

There was nothing outside to compete for interest and his five companions knelt, sat or stood around waiting for the good word. When the computer finally clattered into life and delivered a print-out there was a small drop in tension. They felt they were in business. Something worked.

Bergman studied the tape. Koenig said, 'Well?'

'Some good and some bad.'

Carter said, 'Let's have the good news first. It'll make a change.'

'Behind that hatch, there's a breathable atmosphere. Slightly oxygen rich if anything. There's a power source operating, but some way off. It's an incredibly big and complex structure inside there. A thorough search could take weeks.'

Koenig cut in, 'Do you have any idea what's happened to our communications?'

'That's the bad news. Radiation distortion. As you saw, even the comlocks are affected.'

'Radiation!'

'The ship is saturated with atomic radiation.'

Helena Russell sat back on her heels and looked at Koenig. This was the nightmare hazard always lurking in the background at Moonbase Alpha. They had endless contingency plans and emergency drills to meet any one of a dozen possibilities of failure in the reactors that made life possible on their wandering platform. This was a purpose built, interstellar voyager and it had happened here. She said, 'It's the one thing they'd have no defence for. In spite of all the care they must have taken, it happened to them.'

Bergman said, 'On these readings it's very weak. Too weak to cause genetic damage except over a long period. There's no immediate danger to us.'

'What about the people, Victor?' Koenig had gone to a direct vision port and was looking at the neglected and failing superstructure. If any were alive, they were clearly in no shape to keep the ship fully operational.

'Life signs are confirmed. There is human type life somewhere aboard.'

Koenig came to a decision. There was nothing to be gained by hanging on inside the Eagle. Even if Main Mission sent out a search ship which Kano would eventually try, it was just as likely to end up enmeshed in the same web. He said grimly, 'Okay. Let's go find it.'

Carter and Lowry freed the hatch clips. Auto gear had done a good job. Pressure was equalised. The roomy airlock was like an ante room to the passenger module. As they walked in, a dusty panel glowed at the far end. The planners had assumed that visitors using the entrance might have a language problem and an animated cartoon strip of a humanoid stylised figure gave a clear mime of how to open the hatch.

Years of disuse and lack of maintenance had taken their toll. Carter and Lowry had to heave away to roll it aside. There was a twenty metre square reception area with a desk where a boarding officer would sit and two corridors running off in a 'V'. Overhead light came from ceiling ports set every ten metres. Some had gone out giving areas of shadow.

The left hand corridor was drab but clear. The right hand one had suffered more from neglect and sheets of cladding leaned out askew partly blocking the way ahead.

Koenig said, 'One way or another these corridors must connect up with the main areas of the ship.'

He walked round the desk looking for some 'You are here' route diagram; but there was nothing. He debated about splitting his small party and decided that with the area of search they had to tackle, it was the obvious way. He was conscious that Helena Russell was watching him and he knew for a fact she was not going to like what he had to say.

Unconsciously standing behind the desk to give more official weight to the briefing, he said, 'This is the way we do it. Paul, you and Alan go left at the fork. Watch yourselves. Take no chances. I'll go right with Victor. Helena, you and Lowry stay here close to the Eagle. If there's any trouble with the natives get back inside sharpish and use the ship's armament. If we can't make contact with the Darians, we'll rendezvous back here at 1600 hours. Then it'll be a question of searching round for some local switchgear to override that docking beam. You can be thinking about that one, Helena.'

'I'd rather be with you.'

'I want somebody at base and it's you.'

She knew argument would get her nowhere, but there was no comfort in it. Intuition on a different wave length from Bergman's computer was scenting an indefinable menace more dangerous to them than a radiation hazard. She shivered and moved away to the airlock hatch.

Carter said, 'If they give trouble?'

'Let's hope they understand the purity of our motives. Ready, Victor?'

The two pairs moved off. Bill Lowry joined Helena. 'They'll be all right, Doctor. They can look after themselves.'

'I hope so.'

Koenig and Bergman were soon out of sight hidden by the leaning panels. Progress was easier than they expected. On the whole the floor area was free and the damage was more through lack of regular maintenance than from structural failure. The corridor had once been a smooth tube and there was evidence that a monorail transport system had once been used to ferry the Darians about the hive. Where lighting ports were broken there was a mass of charred circuitry behind the translucent panel.

Koenig said, 'What do you make of it, Victor?'

'It's difficult. Some mechanical failure caused overload. But then it was not a complete blow out. There's certainly a power source operating now and the ship's on a course, whether by design or accident who can say? The survivors may be too few to keep outlying areas up to scratch. But the shell's still sound. It still works.'

'Auto trouble shooters would see to that.'

'There is life. The signs were positive. Human life.'

They had reached a bend in the corridor and Koenig stopped. Ahead, the way was clearer and the eye could travel on through an exercise in perspective to a far distant pin point.

'We're in for a long walk.'

'True, John, but a ship like this is a small city. It's a technical marvel that ranks with the pyramids. It ought to be worth the trouble.'

'That remains to be seen.'

After a fair start Paul Morrow and Carter were meeting an area of general destruction. It was a case of picking a slow path through and over mounds of debris. Whole sections of cladding had peeled from the walls and lay at crazy angles over the path. Alan Carter said, 'If it means anything I'd say it is getting worse. There can't be anything this way.'

'Maybe not, but we might as well check it out.'

'I don't like it. We should be trying to get Eagle One out of the well.'

'One thing at a time. Just get on.'

Carter shrugged and heaved away at a panel that had lodged chest high from wall to wall. Morrow flung himself forward and shouldered the pilot aside. A sliding rumble shook the ground at their feet and lights flipped out for fifty metres. The air filled with choking dust and Carter picked himself up in sudden twilight. As the murk cleared, it was plain there was no further progress to be made. The way ahead was jammed solid.

Carter said, 'That's it, then. Thanks a lot. Next time you can be trail breaker. What now?'

'Back to base.'

Filling in time, Helena Russell had been examining the walls of the area near the airlock. A darker line, like a hair crack, running from a pile of rubble caught her eye and she went close to inspect it.

She called, 'Bill, what do you think about this?'

Bill Lowry, a massive, barrel chested man, looked up and down the seam and then shifted some of the debris from the deck. The crack was vertical from floor to ceiling. Balling a fist like a mallet, he gave it a shrewd thump in the best technical tradition. There was a subdued click as a holding spring disengaged and the faint crack widened to a handsbreadth gap. They took a side each and heaved away.

The two leaves ran soundlessly on a track. Behind the door was a short lighted corridor that turned off abruptly round a corner.

Helena was through and it was left to Lowry to be cautious, 'Shouldn't we wait until the Commander comes back?'

'We should, but we don't have to go far. Just a look round the corner.'

Two steps inside the hatch and there was the first direct evidence of independent life aboard *Daria*. Stopped dead in their tracks they heard a rapid tattoo of quick, light footsteps.

To Helena it sounded like the patter of children's feet. Lowry said, 'Two. At least two,' and drew his laser.

In a sense both were right. The noise increased. There was a panic urgency in it. The two creatures who flung themselves round the corner, eyes wild with fear, were small enough to be children. But they were not children. A male and a female, hairless and bird frail, nude as needles, they could have run from the cover of the trees in a primitive jungle sequence. They were midgets, pigmy people.

Helena Russell felt her skin crawling with disgust. In the sophisticated setting of a deep space craft, they were obscene anachronisms. Then she remembered Bergman's radiation check. Mutation? Had the Darians come to this?

There was another factor to shove the frontiers of revulsion a little farther back. Mouths opening and closing soundlessly, eyes bulging in their skull-like heads, they seemed incapable of making any vocal noises. They were small, mobile symbols of fear and defencelessness made flesh.

Helena began, 'Are you . . . ?'

The male mutant pointed to his mouth and shook his head. He understood, which was amazing in itself and added another small dimension to the pity of it. She said, 'Can you speak?'

There was an emphatic shake from both heads. Then they were still and listening, heads cocked.

'What is it? What's the matter?'

Hearing certainly was keen enough, it was another two seconds before Helena picked up the beat of distant running feet. There was a chase on. They were one jump ahead of a posse.

The female mute whimpered suddenly and made a dash for Lowry. Before he could move, she had thrown herself to the deck at his feet, arms outstretched, fingertips touching the soles of his boots. Submission and appeal could go no further. Her companion looked wildly around and then ran for the open door towards the air lock.

The pursuit was closing in. Before Helena could speak the newcomers had hurled themselves in a body round the bend in the corridor and were coming to a ragged halt as they took in the scene.

There were six and in some ways they were more likely contenders for the honour of ownership. Physically the scale was right. They could have been a random selection of Alphans. But their appearance was barbaric. It gave the lie to any suggestion that *Daria* was in business as a working ship. These were survivors, living off the land and making do with anything they could find. Clothes were a rag bag, roughly made up from some kind of metal cloth and thonging. Makeshift belts carried weapons fashioned from what looked like duralumin ribs. Faces were fierce and bearded. It was a hunting party.

The leading hand, taller and more bizarre than the rest had a white, circular disc on his tunic to identify him. It said HADIN.

Lowry's mute was shivering uncontrollably and edging closer to his feet. There was no doubt that she knew what to expect. There was a moment of balance, neither side wanting to break. Lowry said quietly, 'Doctor, move back slowly . . . then break for it. Get to the Eagle.'

Hadin's fierce gaze was centred on Helena as she stepped back. Lowry moved. The mute wriggled after him trying to keep her hands on his feet.

Lowry's laser roamed over the massed target. But they were

spread out and he could not watch every move. Hidden behind the press, an arm went back for a throw and a short heavy club whipped across the space. The large end thumped home between Lowry's eyes and he was out on his feet before Hadin had jumped in for the pay off.

Lowry was down, stretched out beside the quivering mute. Helena Russell, hands at her sides, could only stand in the centre of a menacing ring and watch Hadin as he walked deliberately towards her. Koenig's attempt to keep her out of the action had misfired and she could only recognise bitterly that it was her own fault. Now she had added another complication for him. She wondered where he was and if the nudge of a sixth sense would let him know.

Koenig and Bergman were a good two kilometres away and approaching an intersection in the long service corridor. There was evidence that here at least the ship was in better repair.

Koenig stopped suddenly and Bergman's face asked his question. Before Koenig could answer, a sound of footsteps could be heard from round the corner. It was enough to explain why Koenig had stopped. For his part, he reckoned he must have picked it up subconsciously before it passed the threshold of attention. Drawing his laser, he went on, keeping close to the wall and then whipping smartly out of cover into the left hand branch of the new passageway.

Two beams of light dropped in bright pools at their feet and they stopped, staring down the empty passage. The noise of footsteps was still approaching. The light beams shifted to the walls and then suddenly flicked over to centre in a dazzling glare on their faces.

Arm over his eyes, Koenig struggled to see out into the corridor. Echoing footsteps were closer. Then he could see and he could only believe that the two bulky figures had sidestepped out of some parallel tunnel.

Bergman, ever one to define a thing for the record, said, 'Radiation suits. They're still working protective drills. Reception party?'

Both figures carried a torch in one hand and a bulbous nosed blaster in the other. Clearly they were taking no chances. Both parties were still, each watching the other.

Koenig, as the visitor, reckoned it was up to him to show

good intentions. Raising his left hand in a mime of greeting, he lowered his laser.

Reaction time for the two Darians was lightning fast. The muzzle of Koenig's gun had barely shifted off target, when they had lifted their blasters and fired as one.

Energy beams flared over the gap. John Koenig and Victor Bergman were out on their feet, waiting for simple mechanical laws to decide which way they fell.

The two suited figures walked slowly forward and stared down at them as though they could not fully understand who the victims might be.

CHAPTER FOUR

Alan Carter was a puzzled man. He called again, 'Lowry! Dr Russell!' There was only an echo to answer him.

Paul Morrow had gone to look along the second tunnel. There was nothing to be seen. He followed Carter through the air lock into the Eagle's passenger module. They checked the command cabin and the freight bay. Nothing.

Suddenly Carter lifted his hand. A small sound of movement was repeated and appeared to come from the deck under one of the transverse squabs in the passenger cabin. Unclipping his laser, he knelt down to check. The terrified face of the male mutant stared out at him.

At precisely the same moment of time, in another part of the metal city, John Koenig's eyes were bringing him a blurred and fragmentary picture of his situation. The flat surface at his back was clearly some kind of slab or table top. Clips at ankle, thigh and chest were holding him flat. His eyes opened, closed, opened again as his conscious mind went in and out of circuit.

Focussing was a problem. Nothing was hard edged. Faces had no precise definition and the room he was in could have been a hangar or a narrow cell. He was only half aware of himself as an observer. It was a dream sequence, as though it was all happening to somebody else. Lighting seemed to flare bright and then dim at the rate of his pulse. Bringing every atom of will to bear, he tried to concentrate and for a moment believed he had it clear. There were only two figures watching him and the suits were familiar. They were the two Darians that he and Bergman had met in the corridor.

That was a small toehold on reality and he tried to build on it. Bergman? That would be Victor Bergman. Where was he then. And Helena? What would happen at Eagle One when he failed to show up? Straining against the clips, he tried to sit up. The effort was too much. Black night filled his eyes and he was off on another trip in the cloud of unknowing.

Helena Russell had no difficulty in knowing where she was, and it was not good. Like all captives through the millennia she was being led into the settlement of the tribe.

She could recognise what it had once been. The spaceborn city had needed a vast hydroponic spread to feed its people and without the care of a trained labour force, vegetation had run amuck. Underfoot, the floor was springy as turf with accumulations of fallen leaves, cycads and exotics towered around in dense groves reaching up to a distant domed ceiling which gave constant sunlight. There was a dank smell of vegetation. They could have walked into a clearing in an Amazonian jungle.

Small goedesic domes, which had once housed the technicians and the monitoring gear, had been stripped out and now served as houses. It was Koenig's nightmare of what could happen to Moonbase Alpha, given a catastrophe.

Having a stable climate, life was clearly lived mainly outside the houses. Gutted consoles were set up as tables. Seats had been roughly fashioned from lengths of duralumin tubing and strips of metal cloth. A woman came up close to stare at her and she saw that the barbaric, ornamental pectoral she was wearing had once been a printed circuit.

Hadin halted the column with a curt gesture. Lowry who had been walking like a zombie was brought savagely to a stop. Directly ahead, the forest clearing ended in a bulkhead which had been kept open for a run of ten metres and reminded Helena of a wayside shrine. Polished slabs lay at the foot and on them were pieces of intricate machinery, whose purpose was no longer known. But each item gleamed and shone. Somebody spent much care to keep them clean and furbished.

There was no doubt that the place had a devotional purpose. Taking pride of place on a central slab was an open book and above it, set in the bulkhead was the picture of a man's face like an ikon. Between the book and the face there was a cavity, a man sized niche that could have held an idol. It was closed by a transparent lid.

It was enough to be going on with. Hadin seemed to rule by gestures. He signalled again. Hands closed on her arms and she was pulled without ceremony to an empty hut. Lowry and the female mute were thrust through the hatch after her. Two guards, swinging clubs took up station at the open door.

Back at the Eagle, Alan Carter was making progress. Squatting on his heels, he had convinced the midget that for the time at least he had nothing to fear and the big stranger was on his side of the fence.

It was a one sided conversation, but Carter persevered. He

said slowly, 'You were here when . . . the others . . . came?'

The mute looked from Carter to Morrow and back again, clenching and unclenching his hands. Then he nodded twice for good measure.

Morrow said, 'Where did they go? Which way? There?' He pointed to the corridor that Koenig had taken.

The mute shook his head and pointed to the wall. It looked like nonsense, but Carter straightened up and walked over to the blank bulkhead. He said, 'He's not kidding, Paul! There's something here and it could be a door.' The mute followed him still pointing and nodding like a clockwork doll.

More sophisticated than Lowry, Paul Morrow searched around for an opening mechanism and found a kick stud under the rubble. The door slid open. Morrow pointed into the corridor, 'This way?'

There was another succession of rapid nods.

'You will show us?'

This was not so popular. Eyes widened with panic and there was a whimper of pure terror.

Morrow said gently, 'You must help us . . . please . . . you will come to no harm. We will protect you.'

The mute looked from one to the other. In his bitter, hunted life, there were no sureties. But something about the two Alphans, not least their obvious compassion, seemed to tip the scale. His nod was minimal. He reckoned he was being a fool to himself. But they were in business. He even led the way through the door.

Coming up for a second time, Koenig found himself in a better situation. Softer fabric at his back told him that he was no longer staked out on his slab. He was in some kind of rest room with a sophisticated decor showing no sign of disrepair.

The most spectacular element in it was seated on a boudoir chair not three metres from his head watching him with large kohl rimmed eyes. Female, elegant, of a flawless, ageless beauty, she wore a shimmering hip-length tabard and broad electrum bangles on her slim wrists.

He was, however, a man with a grouch and his long stare was more challenging than appreciative. Under it, she shifted about, becoming a little uneasy. Koenig said, 'Why did you attack us? We came to help.'

Her voice was clear and bell like, 'Please understand, you were strangers. We found you on our ship. We had to know if your intentions were hostile or not.'

Jacking himself on one elbow, Koenig went on with the hard questions, 'Then why the hell didn't somebody ask?'

'We have probed your mind and the mind of your friend Professor Bergman. We know now that your intentions were good.'

Spoken in that direct, unaffected voice and backed by her serious, candid eyes, it had to be true, but Koenig was still staring hard trying to make sure of her sincerity.

'Who are you?'

'Our people are called Darians.' She pointed to a long mural set in the bulkhead and he saw a great panorama of people thronging the streets of a splendid city. She went on, 'That was our world . . . Daria. I am Kara, Director of Reconstruction on this ship.'

Koenig swung his feet off the couch and stood up. His head was clear, but he felt drained of energy. He took a walk over to the picture and then came back to face her. 'Have you found the rest of my people?'

'Your friend Bergman is resting. For the others, there is some doubt. We are not sure where they are. Do not be anxious. We will find them, but it will take time. You must understand Commander Koenig, apart from this small sector the rest of our ship is still a wilderness.'

She stood up to face him and the movement shook out a pollen cloud of sandalwood. He had to fight a rearguard against conviction. If beauty was truth as the man said, she had to be on the level.

'We picked up your signal.'

'That signal was automatically triggered when certain nuclear reactors on our ship went into a runaway explosion. It has been transmitting ever since.'

That figured. Alpha's own Moon was the victim of a rogue nuclear event. Even the best technology had its failures.

'Ever since when for instance?'

'Since the disaster occurred, a long time, Commander. Nine hundred years. We cannot cut it off.'

It was said in the same simple direct way and he had to believe it, but his mind grappled with the time scale. *Daria* had been a wandering hulk for almost a thousand years. On

Earth that period had seen a fantastic surge of human development. At the beginning William of Normandy was striking across the narrow seas on his English adventure. Man's maximum speed across the face of his planet was the speed of a galloping horse. At the end, there was Confederated Europe and geothermal power and speed was whatever anybody liked to make it.

His own people had gone from a late Iron Age culture to the technocratic civilisation that had built Moonbase Alpha. And *Daria* had gone on ploughing her lonely furrow in the interstellar outback.

Whether Kara could follow his train of thought or not, she could read his bewilderment and deftly changed the subject. 'Only this part of the ship, which housed the high command, was fully shielded. Out of a complement of fifty thousand Darians only fourteen of us survived intact.'

'Fourteen. From so many!'

'Not all died at once, of course. Thousands survived the initial explosions, but they were all sick and doomed, irradiated . . .'

Her voice trailed off. What beauty alone had not been able to do, compassion completed. Koenig was a convinced man. Shocked and sympathetic, he said, 'And we came to offer help. What can we do against suffering on that scale?'

Kara had recovered her composure and was giving him a look which was difficult to define. She said slowly, 'It is true we are way beyond the cry for help which caused you to come here . . . but there *is* a way in which your presence is vital to our survival.'

A faint alarm bell sounded in the depths of Koenig's head, but he was still thinking about *Daria*'s epic passage. He said, 'Anything we can do, we shall do, of course.'

Once committed to the venture, the small mutant seemed to have accepted whatever fate lay ahead. At a quick jog trot, he led Carter and Morrow through a maze of interconnecting passageways into the bowels of the ship.

When he finally stopped at a door which was hanging askew from one broken hinge, Carter drew a sleeve across his sweating forehead. It had been getting steadily warmer and was now a good seventy Celsius.

Morrow said, 'Here?'

The nods were rapid and the little man was looking frightened again. But he went on through the hatch and they followed him out onto an inspection gantry clewed to the wall of the vast garden area where Hadin's people had their home.

Writhing foliage crawled in all directions. Overgrown by creeper, small geodesic domes could be made out dotting the floor. Overhead, some of the immense roof structure with its yellow glaring ports could be seen through the tangle of vegetation. The mute was like a small animal scenting danger. Face raised, he was sniffing the foetid air, body taut as a spring.

He pointed down and Carter found a circular trap with a companion leading to ground level. Once they were down among the foliage, it was anybody's guess where the track lay; but their guide was off again, picking a way through the undergrowth without hesitation. They must have gone half a kilometre before he stopped, shivering with fear.

Carter and Morrow drew their lasers. Morrow bent down and asked in a whisper, 'What is it?' He pointed. Clearly, they were getting close to the action. Ten paces farther on they could hear faintly what he had already heard. There was movement and voices.

The mute was in a pitiable state of fear. As they went forward, he drew back ready to break and run. Morrow mimed that he would be safe and was to come with them, but he shook his head, backing off into the bush. Then suddenly, he turned on his heel and vanished.

Morrow was half-tempted to follow, but Carter was anxious to get on. 'Leave him, Paul. He did all we asked. He got us here. Let's see what it's all about.'

Moving cautiously, they went for the voices. Fifty metres farther on, they were at the edge of the clearing and some ceremony was afoot centred on what could only be an altar and a shrine.

It was as savage a scene as any enacted in a jungle clearing, in spite of some of the technical junk that was in use. Primitives were busy with a tribal ritual.

There was a semicircle of men and women round the temple area. Attended by guards, Helena Russell, Bill Lowry and a small female pigmy were being escorted out of their prison cell. At the edge of the circle, the leading hand who was organising the ceremony stopped short and pointed to the mute. She was seized. The circle opened and she was thrust inside.

She stood where she was put, too petrified by fear to move. But there was no sign of pity or compassion on any face, male or female, in the assembly. There was a waiting silence, a greediness for some kind of sacrifice to come. A very old man, hardly able to walk, dressed in a bizarre, shroud-like garment of metal cloth with printed circuits and strings of transistors hanging around him like amulets, came slowly from a geodisic dome and approached the intent circle.

It opened to let him pass. Hands stretched out in front of him, he tottered slowly towards the small, naked figure. As his fingers touched her head, her mouth opened in a soundless scream. The gnarled hands of the oldster moved over her hairless crown and to her shoulders. The crowd waited, breathless, expectant, knowing the outcome, but wanting the sanctity of an official pronouncement from their *shaman*. It came in a hoarse shout from a mouth of broken teeth. 'Mute!'

It was the signal for audience participation. Taken up from every side in a fierce chant, the roar of 'Mute! Mute!' rang round the clearing.

Noise broke the spell of terror holding the victim to the spot. She darted for the ring of watchers with a vain hope of getting out. But two guards were in with a rush and seized her by her arms. At a run, they dragged her to the shrine. A third had swung open the transparent door of the cavity in the wall and she was thrown forward and in. When the hatch was closed, she could be seen clawing insanely at the smooth glass.

The operator was making ritual signs of profound respect to a boxlike control console. Everything must be done with correct procedure. When he finally pressed a red button and stood clear, the crowd roared again 'Mute! Mute!'

Intense light glowed in the capsule. For a beat the scrabbling intensified. Then the frantic body was still and seemed to be shrinking. With the crowd's shout going on like a rhythmic countdown, it thinned and eteliolated to a wisp of glowing gas and then it was gone.

Excluded from the circle, Bill Lowry and Helena Russell had no clear idea of what was going on.

Lowry said, 'What are they doing in there?'

'I don't know. I wish we could see.'

There was a hush and a small surge in the crowd that gave

her a clear view to the dying glow in the capsule. The mute had gone and no crystal ball was needed to tell where.

Before she could react to the full horror of it, the crowd was looking at Hadin for the next move. Hadin lifted his club. It was Lowry.

Dragged into the ring, Lowry put up a fight, but there was no ghost of a chance. Held rigid, he was presented to the oldster. The crooked fingers touched his hair, then his face. Lowry's tunic, already torn was ripped off and the exploring hands checked the torso, then the arms. At the left hand he suddenly stopped with a cackle of triumph and one of his helpers held the arm out for all to see.

Relic of an accident with loading gear, Lowry had lost the first joint of the index finger on his left hand. The old man's shout rang out, 'Mute!'

The crowd rocked and chanted, 'Mute! Mute! Mute!'

Real fear had gotten through to Lowry. He knew he was in a terminal situation. His shouts turned to a scream of despair as he was dragged kicking and struggling to the cavity and manhandled inside.

Carter and Morrow had worked closer. Now they could see clearly what was going on. The operator shoved down the stud and Lowry's struggles were over.

Laser in hand, Carter was on his way when Paul Morrow pulled him back.

'But Lowry. Look what they've done to Bill Lowry!'

'Hold it. We can't help him now. Helena's right in the middle of those bastards. What chance would she have if we start shooting now? We can't get to them all before somebody gets to her.'

Angrily, Alan Carter said, 'We can't just do nothing!'

'Wait!'

The glow died. Lowry was gone. Alan Carter checked his laser. Before the charges ran out, there would be many to accompany him on his journey. Grim faced, he watched the crowd settle for another round of ritual.

Helena Russell shrugged off the hands that were aiming to force her into the circle. She was afraid, deeply and utterly afraid, but she was not going to be dragged screaming and shouting to the edge of the grave. Head tall, her face composed, she forced herself to walk, unhelped, into the centre of the circle.

She remembered Everyman's journey. At the last, he had come to accept the thesis that this was the one thing that had to be done alone. The unique bundle of experience and personality that had made her look out on the world from one pair of eyes was due to close its ledger. Even if John Koenig had been here, they would have had to cross the last barrier one at a time. It was harsh, but it was true, and in the context of the immense universe, it was unimportant. For her, their long seeking for a homecoming was at an end. She hoped he was safe and that he would go on. But she had to close her mind to that. Otherwise she would not be able to stay calm.

The grotesque hands were stroking her hair. They ran hungrily over her face. Other hands were roughly stripping off her tunic, belt, slacks. Then her thick soled boots. The oldster's hands went on with their remorseless check.

In spite of the warmth in the air and her iron will not to show the fear that was driving her almost insane, she was shivering with involuntary muscular tremors that were outside any hope of control.

The old man was standing in front of her, staring fixedly into her eyes, showing his vile teeth. Medical training died hard and one part of her mind judged that good medicare would have them tidied up for the sake of his digestive tract.

The mouth opened wider and her brain gagged. For a split second she thought she would fall and then she recognised he was calling a different tune.

The word he had yelled with a gust of bad breath was, 'Clear!' and the crowd had taken it up. To give them their due, they seemed pleased about it. Maybe the savage destruction of mutants had been forced on them by a will to survive.

The shout went round the circle again, 'Clear! Clear!'

The old man had a new piece of ceremony to initiate. When there was silence, he called out, 'Prepare to summon the spirits.'

A woman had pushed out of the crowd holding a metal cloth tabard and a plaited belt. She knelt down respectfully and offered them on extended arms.

Suddenly conscious that she was the only complete nude on the set, Helena slipped on the tabard and fastened the belt. Another woman came forward and took her by the hand. This time she was being led rather than driven, but the destination was the same. She was taken back to the geodesic hut, that had served as a prison.

Out in the bush, Carter said, 'So far so good, but I still don't like it. We have to get her out of there. What does the old bastard mean about the spirits?'

'I'd say she passes the local test, but the spirits have to be consulted. How long do spirits take? We'll work round there and see how close we can get.'

Koenig found he was unable to make up his mind. Whether it was the lingering after effect of the session under the Darian probe, or simply that the data coming into his mind were so finely balanced that decision was, anyway, difficult, he could not say. One thing was for sure, it was making him irritable and Kara's eloquent eyes did nothing to help.

When talking to her, he felt he had to believe her. But evidence from the semi-derelict hulk of the vast spacer did not entirely gell. In nine hundred years, a small crew with a power source and a lot of sophisticated equipment still functioning ought to have done some sorting out.

Then there was Helena and the rest of the landing party. In spite of Kara's disclaimer, he had a hunch that, on this one, she was being evasive. But it was gut judgement. Everything she said and the way she said it marked her out as Truth's own sister.

Bergman joined him, received a frank, radiant smile of welcome from Kara and said, 'This is an amazing ship, John, and not just in size. Medical techniques are way ahead of anything we have. Their mind scanner taps into memory banks. When she set out from Daria she must have been one of the wonders of the Galaxy.'

Kara smiled again. She liked it. He was more appreciative than Koenig, who refused to be charmed. She said frankly, 'Coming from a man with your great powers of mind, that is praise indeed, Professor. Perhaps we have things to teach you. But I am sure you also have knowledge to give us.'

Koenig broke in on the détente with a jarring practical note. 'I must talk with your Commander. Where is he to be found?' At the same time, he took a step towards the hatch.

Kara proved she could move smartly and still be graceful about it. She was on her feet in a lissom glide and between

Koenig and the hatch. He had a flash of intuition that she did not want him wandering about the command suite without a guide. Which could only mean that there was something he was not supposed to see. But her ready speech was all agreement, 'Of course. Our Commander will be anxious to meet you and thank you for your response to our signal. Follow me.'

Daria's Supreme Commander was nearer than they expected and might well have been on his way to make a courtesy call. He was at the end of a short corridor, turning from a massive door which showed signs of heat damage and which he had just closed. He was tall, had the same ageless look that characterised Kara, and was dressed in a steel grey fluted tabard. He was an urbane, polished type; but the eyes were hard and direct as he stared at the approaching Alphans.

If Koenig had been with the party in the hydroponics spread, he would have recognised him as the living model of the barbarian's ikon.

His voice was cultured and positive, 'Welcome. I am Neman, Commander of this ship.'

Koenig dispensed with formalities and went right to the heart of the matter, 'Have you found the rest of our people?'

'Unfortunately, no.'

Bergman said, 'We planned to rendezvous back at our ship.'

The steely eyes turned to give him the full treatment and the unhurried voice said, 'There's no one near here, but it's possible they are looking for you.'

Neman's eyes shifted to Kara and although there was no flicker of a signal, Koenig felt they had exchanged some communication. Neman went on, 'Believe me, we are doing our best.'

It was all too calm. Koenig said angrily, 'And not succeeding, dammit!'

Neman's cool was unruffled. He said, 'Commander, I understand your concern for your people. But you must also understand that we are few in number.' He turned back to the closed door and spun a hand wheel in the centre panel. Holding bolts slid clear and the door sagged open on strained hinges. He waved them forward. 'See. This will show you the scale. The ship is huge.'

It was true. They already knew it, but they followed him out to a high gantry set on the side of the power house which had shoved *Daria* over the reaches of space.

The sheer size of the machinery and the immense area of the vaulted chamber were staggering. He had made his point. Hands on the guard rail, Koenig looked about him. Only a fraction of the gear was functional. For the rest, a works team of hundreds with the backing of a planet-based workshop would be hard pressed to put it back into order.

At that level, he had to be convinced. He said quietly, 'All right. I take your point. I understand you have problems.'

Neman said, 'Be so good as to follow me.'

Dwarfed by the scale of *Daria*'s devastated heartland, the group moved along the gantry. Koenig walked beside Neman and the Darian Commander suddenly opened up on another tack, 'As Commander of the Alpha base on the Moon, your people accept your decisions?'

'That is correct. Why do you ask?'

Neman looked closely at his partner, 'First, Commander, has it occurred to you how very similar our situations are. This ship, your Moon, both seeking an end to their long journeys. Both of us victims of an unforeseen disaster.'

Koenig was not sure of the drift, but he reckoned he was giving nothing away by agreeing to that, 'Yes. We have that in common.'

'You know that this ship was virtually destroyed, that few of our people survived – but do you know what our mission was?'

Again, Koenig was on the receiving end of a direct look and Neman went on to surprise him with a little Earth history.

'You may recall from the early days of your Earth culture there is the record of a ship in which the life of a doomed world was preserved?'

Bergman had been walking close enough to hear the conversation and said, 'You mean the Ark?'

'Indeed, Professor. And I tell you that this ship has a similar function – to preserve the life and skills of the Darian race.'

They had reached another massive door. Neman opened it and they went through into a corridor. Kara said, 'You see our planet, *Daria*, no longer exists. We who set out on this voyage were the chosen survivors of our race.'

Neman said, 'Is it not true that your own planet Earth may also no longer exist?'

Where the conversation was heading was a mystery. Koenig said shortly, 'It's possible.'

'Your community on Moonbase Alpha may be all that is left of Earth civilisation?'

'That, too, is possible.'

'But a possibility you dare not ignore?'

'Maybe, but it is also the incentive that spurs our will to survive.'

'And will you survive?' Neman seemed to have come to his key question and walked more swiftly to a smaller hatch which he opened and went through.

When all were in, Kara closed the door. It was a familiar scene to Koenig. He was in a Command Centre, not unlike Main Mission. There was a command console, supporting desks round the perimeter in a horse shoe. He could imagine Neman sitting there calling the shots as he conned *Daria* on her interstellar passage.

Beyond the central command area there was another larger spread, seen through a panoramic window where several Darians were moving about on routine chores.

Koenig continued the conversation, 'We make it a rule not to anticipate the future. Our concern is with the present and for the present, yes, we will survive.'

'But for how long? Your Moon is lost, at the mercy of all random forces of deep space. There will come a time when your resources are not enough. They will fail you. Your people will start to die. All will perish.'

For the honour of Moonbase Alpha, Bergman said, 'We have some way to go before that happens.'

Neman and Kara exchanged glances and Neman said, 'Commander Koenig. We are coming to the end of a voyage of a thousand years. In spite of all the devastation you have seen, our main drive has maintained a steady thrust. We know where we are. The ship is programmed to reach our destination, a virgin planet where the Darian civilisation can begin again.'

This piece of information opened up a whole new line of thinking. Koenig was already well ahead when Neman put it into words, 'Don't you understand me? You are operating on blind chance and statistics are against you. We are offering your community a *guarantee* of survival.'

Koenig looked at the two Darians. It was an offer to climb off a drifting raft onto a passing ship with a port on the chart. But he felt instinctively that there was some collateral that he had missed. He was still searching for the drawback as Neman warmed to his theme and went on, 'Join us. Share our future in the new world which awaits our arrival.

'I know you are concerned for the rest of your party. I shall personally take charge of the search. In the meantime, please consider our offer.'

CHAPTER FIVE

After an interval to recharge their emotional batteries, the crowd in the settlement had reformed in an expectant circle round their shrine. Morrow and Carter were still fifty metres from their objective when the action was rejoined. The medicine man was not through with Helena. Another ritual was being set up.

Hadin called to the guards. Two of them entered the geodesic dome. Helena Russell, pale and strained, but still proud and erect came out between her escorts.

They marched her through the ring to stand before the altar where the oldster was already working himself to a frenzy. Voice edged with hysteria he croaked, 'Here in the Sacred Shrine of knowledge we dedicate this perfect body. We pledge her in the spirit of true science. We pledge her in the light of clear knowledge and vow and affirm that she is free of the Mute whom we abhor in all his manifestations.'

Morrow said bitterly, 'Everybody has to invent the devil to shrug off his own guilt. What do they want from her?'

'How long do we wait?'

'Get in closer. We can't afford to miss.'

The old man was looking at Neman's battered picture and he addressed it for his incantation, 'This we pledge on the sacred book of Neman, maker of men, father of spirits. To you, Neman, we the survivors of Level Seven, pledge this offering.'

Hadin strode forward and shoved down a stud on the console. Then he backed away a pace at a time and an awed silence fell on the arena. There was not long to wait. All lights suddenly dimmed.

Carter thumped Morrow's arm and took off, bent double, running for the back of the crowd. There was a nervous stir from the assembly, the pay off was close. Helena was looking wildly about her, wanting to face whatever it was. A sound from the bulkhead had her whirling round. A door was sliding open beside the destructor niche.

It was difficult to see what was going on. Carter and Morrow were in the rear rank unnoticed. They could have been beating a drum and no eye would have turned from the shadowy shape that appeared in the aperture.

Helena, lips dry, was backing away. Hadin moved in and shoved her violently forward so that she staggered, missed her footing and fell full length on the peaty floor.

The opening was wide enough to admit two figures side by side. They marched forward into the clearing. Darkened visors glinted in the dim light, bulky radiation suits hid any human outline. They were grotesque and horrific shapes to the barbarians.

Morrow and Carter were elbowing a way through the press. They saw Helena trying to get to her feet and the two zombies stump up to her and take an arm apiece to lift her. Clearly, they had no fear of the locals nor any interest except in the victim.

Morrow yelled, 'Stun beam. We might hit Helena,' and he and Carter were through into the inner space. At last it dawned on the barbarians that there was an anti-social faction about, trying to disrupt the ceremony and some ran forward to intercept. They fell like ninepins as both lasers fired.

The two Darians had reached their hatch and turned to check out the commotion. It was the first good news that had come her way for some time and Helena's voice was ecstatic, 'Alan . . . Paul . . . !'

But Hadin was not finished. The ceremony was going awry and it was his responsibility. He charged in like a tank and grabbed Carter in a tackle that brought them both to the deck. The Darians had seen enough. It was not their business. The survivors of Level Seven could knock seven kinds of hell out of each other in their absence. Helena was struggling to get free and they concentrated on dragging her through the hatch.

Hadin's strength was too much for Carter. He was being slowly throttled. Using the last surge of energy he could raise, he got minimum movement for his right hand and swung his laser in a short, vicious arc to clump home on the side of Hadin's head. Then he was struggling to free himself from the dead weight of a stunned man.

Paul Morrow had been jumped by three Survivors and his only small advantage was that he knew who he was and in the dim light they were confused about each other. Swinging his laser like a club, he had two down and one to go when another one took him from behind and brought him down. He was a minute getting back into the action and when he was free to look around, Helena was disappearing through the hatch.

He made a marksman's job of it, cradling his laser on his left forearm and the bright beam arced out for a dead centre hit on the left-hand marker's black visor. There was no argument, the Darian reeled out of the trap and folded. Alan Carter crossed the line of fire, charging in to take the other one, but the Darian was ready, fired once and a blinding asterisk of white light blossomed on Carter's chest.

The Alphan went face down in a crumpled heap and the Darian was away hauling Helena along by main force. The doors began to slide together. Paul Morrow ran for the closing gap and was in with a fine fraction to spare.

The doors closed at his back cutting off a confused scene. The oldster was quietly frothing through his broken teeth, beyond the reach of question and answer. Helped by a couple of his guards, Hadin was sitting up fingering a weal on the side of his head. Confusion was absolute. The only non-moving figure was Alan Carter who lay where he had dropped.

John Koenig and Victor Bergman had been left alone with the proposition hanging in the air. It was tempting, there was no doubt about that and maybe the Alphans would welcome it. Koenig knew it would depend a lot on how he presented the idea and there were a number of angles to get clear before he could begin to make up his mind. He would have liked Helena's clear headed views and where she might be was a nagging, background worry.

Bergman said, 'It comes down to this. If we throw in our lot with them, they allow us to share their new world.'

'It isn't as simple as that, Victor. Our people would have to move from a secure, healthy environment to the hazards of this ship. I'd need a lot of data on that before I could recommend it.'

'There isn't a lot of time. The Moon is going to run out of Eagle range.'

'Exactly. A hurried decision could take us out of the frying pan into the fire with a vengeance. They won't reach that planet for a hundred years. A *hundred* years, Victor. It's a long time. None of us would be around to see it.'

'True, but we could rehabilitate massive sectors of this ship.

Start families. Prepare our people for the future. It's a serious proposal, John. We can't go on for ever as we are. We are wanderers, they have a programmed planetfall ahead. Neman has offered us a free hand to check his offer. He said we were welcome to use the data banks in his Command Centre.'

'It would mean abandoning Alpha at short notice, maybe only time for one trip. Then there would be no turning back. Resources pooled. All right, Neman's off looking for the rest, we'll look at it. See what the chances are that we could complete this voyage with the Darians.'

'We owe it to our people, if there's a real chance.'

'I know that, but I want the facts.'

It was Bergman's province to find them and when they reached the Command Centre, Koenig left him to it. Neman seemed to be as good as his word. There was no interference. A few Darians were still moving about in the operations room, but they had the key desks to themselves. Even Kara had disappeared.

Bergman settled down at the computer console. First things first, he reckoned he should estimate the viability of the food chain. There would be over three hundred extra mouths to feed and more in a family situation.

Koenig took the command seat. Before he did anything else, he wanted to know how his Eagle could be sprung from the trap. There was a long silence that lengthened to a half hour. Victor Bergman took a print-out from the computer and studied it, frowning. He crossed the floor to Koenig who had his desk top covered with working diagrams.

Koenig looked up, 'I think I've located the airlock mechanism. No great problem. We should be able to fix it for controlled entry and exit.'

There was no reply and he saw that Bergman was not looking happy.

'What's wrong?'

'I'm not sure . . . We know that the Darians are human on the same biological pattern as ourselves. Their food requirements should be similar to ours.'

'So?'

'Well . . .' Bergman put a data sheet on the desk, 'These are the staples we use to provide food on Alpha. They're processed and recycled, of course, to make them palatable, but the basic ingredients have to be there.' He flapped down another sheet and Koenig arranged them side by side.

Bergman went on, 'These are the Darian requirements. They have a different preparation system, but the basic ingredients ought to be the same.'

Koenig studied the analysis. He said, slowly, 'No basic proteins, no amino acids or trace elements, no enzyme variants ... the Darians can't support life on these.'

'That's what I'd say. But the Darian computer supplied the figures. I've checked. There's no mistake. There are no reserves of those elements anywhere on this ship.'

If Bergman said so then it was true, but it made no kind of sense. Koenig said, 'But Victor, what are you saying? You can't get round the plain fact that they've kept themselves alive for nine hundred years.'

'Not on these resources, they haven't.'

'Have you checked on the recycling procedures themselves?'

'Yes. At that stage every one of those essential elements is present ... and there's a steady renewal.'

Koenig was already half way there and met Bergman's eyes over the desk. 'But if they have no reserves on the ship ... how?'

'I said they had no reserves of those elements on the ship ... but that's not strictly correct. There *is* one source where they could find high grade replacements – a *human* source.'

'The top slot of the food chain. Bodies?'

'There's no other theory to fit, John. Living human bodies.'

One body that would not lie down was stirring painfully on the peaty floor of the arena in the barbarians' camp. Alan Carter opened his eyes, groaned, and tried to sit up. The scene around him wavered, split into double vision and settled again.

Hadin, beside himself with anger at the disruption of the ceremony, noticed the move and planted a shrewd kick in the Alphan's groin. Pain exploded in Carter's tired head and he dropped back to the deck. Two guards ran in and grabbed him from either side, hauling him to his feet to face the oldster, who had been muttering to himself, but now had a new target. Shoving his face close to Carter's he fairly spat out, 'Defiler of truth! Defiler of this sacred place! Killer of the spirit! *Enemy of Neman!*'

It was not strictly true. Morrow had been the marksman and

he was currently having trouble finding his way through the maze of corridors that the Darian had entered. But Carter was not in a mood to argue. As the pain subsided and his vision cleared, a red tide of anger burned out the lingering effects of the stun beam. He had taken enough. If he could get his hands on a weapon he would start with Hadin and blast every living thing in sight.

Almost as the thought formed, he saw where there was one. The Darian was still lying where he had fallen and there was a blaster in the clip on his belt.

The oldster was uttering pure gibberish, but the crowd of survivors were drinking it all in, waiting for the pay off line which would send another stranger to the death chamber. Backing away from Carter, the old man approached the Darian and began to wave his hands over the body. He was asking for forgiveness, explaining that Level Seven had not been involved in the act of sacrilege.

It was effective. The Darian moved. Reaction was out of all proportion. Some barbarians fell on their knees. A woman began a keening wail. Others backed off. The oldster stood his ground. After all, if there was any credit to be had, it should accrue to him. He said, 'Spirit of science forgive us . . . Spirit of knowledge protect us . . . Spirit of Neman preserve us.'

Carter's guards, as bemused as anybody else, had slackened their grip. He wrenched himself clear and took off in a sprint start for the Darian who had gotten himself off the deck and was sitting up. Before the man had time to realise, Carter was on him and had the blaster out of its clip.

There was a yell from the survivors. More sacrilege. More sin to expiate. They were rushing forward to protect the representative of the gods as Carter heaved him to his feet and jammed the blaster in his spine.

Carter shouted, 'This is no spirit! Do you hear me? Look for yourselves.' With his free hand, he ripped open the helmet seals and tore it from the Darian's head.

It stopped the rush. There was a gasp from all hands. Bewilderment was almost comic as they stared at the human head sticking out of the bulky radiation suit.

Carter went on, 'They have deceived you. This is only a man. A man like you!'

Expressions were changing. Nobody likes to be proved a

fool. The Darian could read the signs, he tried to back away, fear growing in his eyes. The blaster shifted station and the muzzle ground into his left ear.

Carter said, 'Your turn, Spirit, tell them how it is. Tell them what kind of spirit you are.'

There was no answer and Carter shoved the blaster hard home, 'Don't push me, Spirit. I'd rather blow your fool head off than not. Tell them the truth or I'll throw you to them.'

'No . . . no . . . please!'

'Then tell them!'

It was no easy assignment. The Darian's voice was choked. 'It is true . . .'

'Louder, Spirit. They won't get the message.'

This time it was a hysterical shout, 'It is true . . . I am no spirit!'

The effect on Hadin and his survivors was strange. Suddenly they knew it was true and a whole area of their culture pattern was in ruins. They began to move forward slowly. It was doubtful whether they separated Carter and the Darian in their thinking. They wanted vengeance for all the blood that their own superstition had spilled over the years.

Carter had a neck lock on the Darian and the man was struggling, 'Let me go.'

There was not much time. If Hadin and his crew got to him, there would be no chance of question and answer, 'You know where the rest of my people are?'

'Yes, yes.'

'You will take us there?'

'Yes.'

Hadin was only three paces off, swinging his club. Carter said, 'Wait,' and shifted the blaster for a point blank target on the barbarian's ID disc.

Hadin stopped. It was crystal clear that Carter would rather fire than not and even a body twitch would tip the balance. He held still with his club in mid swing as Carter went on, 'It's time you knew the score. This man will take us to the place of false spirits. Then, at last, you will know the whole truth. Who will follow?'

There was a pause as the crowd digested it. A lot had happened in a short time and the implications went deep. But they were not basically stupid. Carter could sense the tide turning his way. He took a calculated risk and turned his back on them, prodding the Darian with the blaster and driving him through the open hatch. Behind him, there was a stir of movement. When he looked around, the survivors of Level Seven, led by Hadin, were moving forward to meet their destiny.

Confronted by the two data sheets and Koenig's hard, challenging stare, Kara showed no sign of confusion. She glanced at the figures, crumpled the papers and tossed the ball neatly into a disposal bin. It was a gesture of finality. The chips were down.

Koenig asked harshly, 'Is it true?'

'Does it matter where we get those elements from?'

'It matters!'

The brilliant eyes never wavered, 'We would have told you.'

'When? When it was too late for us to alter our decision?'

There was no answer, he went on, 'A *civilised* people . . . why?'

She was stung to a reply, short, but all embracing in her book, 'To live!'

'The end justifies the means! Doesn't it also matter *how* you live?'

'Our experience on this ship has taught us the truth. The only ultimate truth. Survival.'

'You cannot justify using the living bodies of your own people on a plea of survival. Who are the Darians to be that important?'

'Not our own people. How could we? There are only fourteen true Darians on this ship. But others . . .'

'Others?' It was a new piece of information and Koenig rapped out his question.

'Yes. There are others. They exist out there in the radioactive wilderness. They are the descendants of the original survivors. Only the top executive team were in the fully screened command area. The rest had to be left to die, there was no other action we could take. It was twenty years before we knew that some still survived. You cannot understand what we found when it was possible to make a search. A million years of civilisation . . . wiped clean in less than a generation. What survived were degenerate creatures, mutants, savage cannibals.'

The proposition was clear enough. Anywhere, at all times and in all places, civilisation was hard won and hard kept, a thin veneer that could peel off and leave man naked to start over as a walking ape. But this time, there was a reservoir of knowledge that had not been lost and could have been used.

'Why didn't you help them?'

'We could not reveal our presence. They would have overwhelmed us and all would have been lost. But we tried to help them to survive. We taught them the rudiments of science. We gave them a god to believe in. A god who showed them how to preserve only the fittest of the stock. The weak, the sick, the mutants were . . .'

Koenig's contempt was cutting, '. . . were weeded out and used as human fodder for your converters. Recycled to keep the godlike Darians in business.'

For the first time, Kara was defensive. 'That only became a policy decision when our own vital resources gave out. You still refuse to understand . . . we were the only true Darians left. We had to survive!'

Given the premise, the action had a logic, but Koenig said with heavy sarcasm, 'You Darians put a high value on yourselves!'

She said quickly, 'You think we did all this for our own *personal* survival . . . so that Neman and I and the others could continue to live?'

'What else?'

'There is a greater survival. Come. You will see what it is.'

Beside the computer bank there was a sealed unit which Bergman had not been able to unlock and Kara had to fetch Neman himself to operate a dual mechanism to which they both carried half the key.

In her absence, Victor Bergman said slowly, 'What they have done is terrible, but there is a certain harsh logic in it. The question is whether our people are prepared to integrate with such a community. We would change. They would change. Change in itself cannot be resisted, it is the very business of life.'

'But we have to make the best choice we can. I am not satisfied that this is the best choice. Moonbase Alpha is finite. I accept that. But our community is in good heart. We don't have to accept a bad risk. Not yet . . .'

Kara was back again, followed by Neman. Both moved to the sealed unit and used their keys. Kara stood clear like a conjuror's assistant and left the top hand to show the marvel.

As the panel slid away, the glowing interior dominated the drab surroundings. Glistening clusters of fibrous material were coiled in the familiar pattern of a double helix, the structure of the genetic core of the life principle. It was a gene bank.

Neman said, 'Our mission is to survive this voyage, not for our own sake, but for this . . . our gene bank. It contains the undamaged genetic material of our race.'

Koenig said, 'The Double Helix . . . it is also the basic genetic brick of our species.'

'Then you will understand how important this is to us. We have kept it screened from the radiation that irreparably damaged our people. With it we can build up our race again. Pure, healthy Darians. When that is done we will be ready to leave the stage.'

Kara said, 'That is why we need you, John Koenig. You have the resources we need to complete our voyage and save our race from extinction.'

There was no doubt on that score. Koenig could see that the Darians needed the Alphans. But there were two sides to the coin. Did the Alphans need the Darians that much or at all?

'You have managed pretty well in your fashion without us.'

Neman said frankly, 'Not for much longer. The mutant survivors are dying faster than they can replace themselves. If they die, then all life on this ship perishes and with it a million years of civilisation. Can you be content to allow that? Join us, John Koenig, put an end to this terrible thing we've had to do. It will guarantee our survival and your future.'

'We shall consider it. As of now, we do nothing until you have found the rest of our people.'

Kara's quick look to Neman was her first unguarded act. It did nothing to reassure Koenig. He spun on his heel and stalked out of the Command Centre followed by Bergman.

Alan Carter was prodding his Darian in front of him and Hadin's band, though looking anxious, was still streaming behind in a ragged column.

Ahead of the field, Paul Morrow was using commando techniques, slamming open doors and going in with a rush to cover empty rooms with his questing laser. For his money, he could have become the only living creature on *Daria*. Rounding an elbow bend in a corridor that had a better maintained look than anything yet, his theory took a knock. There was at least one other. A Darian had walked smartly out of a hatch and was less than three metres off, a surprised man.

The Darian's mouth opened for a warning yell which was stillborn. Morrow fired from the hip and black night filled the Darian's eyes. He was still falling when Koenig and Bergman appeared from another door.

Morrow said, 'Commander! He would have raised the alarm. They've got Helena . . . she must be somewhere around here!'

'She was with Lowry. Where's Lowry?'

'Lowry bought it!'

'Carter?'

'I don't know. He was hit. We got separated back there. But Helena was brought this way. They gave her a bad time.'

Koenig's jaw set like a trap. Neman was still holding out on them. He must have known what was happening. In a cold fury, he went for the Command Centre.

Followed by Morrow and Bergman he stormed through the hatch. Neman was nowhere in sight. Kara was working at the computer desk. She looked up, suddenly anxious, it was clearly a hostile visit.

'What is this . . . ?'

Speech cut off. Koenig had reached her and plucked her out of the seat, one hand clamped over her mouth. Hauling her head back, so that he could look into her eyes, he made the position deadly plain.

'Listen carefully, Kara. We know how you have used those people out there . . . how you have exploited them. All right, that's your problem and theirs. We make no judgement. But right now you Darians have taken one of our people, a woman. You will tell me where she is or one Darian executive ends her long voyage here and now.'

Fear showed in Kara's eyes. It was all true. He would do what he said. He felt her frenzied nod of agreement against his hand and released the pressure.

Hardly able to speak she said, 'Come with me.'

There was another door in the corridor from the gantry to the Command Centre and when the hatch was back, a waft of formaldehyde met them. It was a medicentre and one dedicated for special use. A line of mortuary tables carried four naked bodies preserved under a blue aseptic light. Not only were they dead, they projected the aura of absolute death. They had a curious, caved in, gutted look.

Bergman was on to it in a flash. 'Transplant donors! Used as needed!'

Koenig hardly heard, he was fully committed elsewhere. Naked as any needle and strapped to an investigation slab, Helena Russell was wired up to a spread of monitors. The Barbarians in the cellar might be content with a manual check; but the sophisticates of the afterguard wanted a detailed scan before they used any part of her in their repair and refit programme.

Kara ran past him, flipped switches along the control panel and a rash of green tell-tales winked live. Helena stirred and groaned.

Koenig's voice was quiet, but loaded with death, 'What have you done to her?'

Hastily, knowing she was as near the end of the line as she had ever been, Kara said, 'She's reviving. Investigation procedures. She has not been harmed.'

'Remove the leads.'

Koenig knelt by the bed and smoothed a swathe of honey blonde hair from Helena's forehead. Her eyes were closed, but her breathing was deep and regular. The sleeping and the dead. What would he have done if Helena had been dead?

He stood up. 'Give her your tabard.'

When it was done, Kara seemed smaller and older. The face was the same, but the body was seamed with faint marks of scar tissue.

Koenig said, 'What is this place?'

Shrinking from him, Kara said evasively, 'We Darians are sterile. Ever since the catastrophe we have had to prolong life by artificial means.'

Bergman said again, 'Transplant surgery!'

Her face confirmed it. This time Koenig heard and understood. Rage almost choking him, he said, 'This butchery! This is how you cling on to your lives? Is there no limit to what you Darians will commit in the sacred name of survival?'

'Could we have done otherwise?'

Another angle had occurred to Koenig, 'Was this the future you had in mind for the Alphans? To keep you Darians alive for the last lap of your journey? Was that the plan?'

He got an answer, but not from Kara. Neman and a Darian

guard had come in unnoticed. They had blasters covering the Alphan party. Neman said, 'Yes.'

The nearer he got to the heartland of the great ship, the more trouble Carter was having with his column. At the gantry, skirting the fantastic power house, he had to prop his Darian against a bulkhead to rally the stragglers.

'What sort of people are you? Do you want to turn back now that you know the truth? Come on, Spirit, shout it out. Tell them there's nothing to fear.'

The Darian mustered a croak. He was afraid of Carter and afraid of the confrontation that lay ahead. But he rightly judged he would have no part in the ongoing action unless he did what the Alphan asked.

'You have nothing to fear. We are men like yourselves. The last of the Darians.'

Hadin and the survivors came forward. If anything, it was the fear in the Darian's voice that convinced them. A true Spirit ought to be past concern for its own skin. There was a growl of assent. Carter moved on. There was an open hatch and the Darian went for it. He muttered, 'Now we are entering the Command Sector.'

It was brighter, clearer than anywhere they had yet seen. Here, at least, it was possible to believe that *Daria* was a working ship. Two Darians, a man and a woman, leaving the operations area, turned into the corridor and saw the motley rabble filling the way from edge to edge and stood rooted in shock. After so many centuries, the crew had marched aft to see the skipper and from the look of the Alphan at the head of the column it was no social visit.

There was a pause while Hadin's faction stopped also to look at the trim, uniformed Darians.

The Darians moved first. Unarmed, they made a run for it. Any psychologist would have told them it was the worst thing they could have done. They had put themselves on the level of the fleeing and hunted mutes. The survivors responded like a pack of hounds and were away, sweeping past Carter.

He let them go, turned his Darian to face the wall and clubbed him smartly with the bulbous end of the blaster. 'Apologies, Spirit. But I don't want you getting up to any dangerous practices.' Then he was away after Hadin.

In the transplant room, Neman was using his tactical advantage to push his case. Earnestly, he said, 'Think of it . . . all of you executive Alphans. Unlimited life. Our techniques are refined and perfected, this is no false claim. When the voyage ends, you will still be alive and your future assured.'

Icy voiced, Koenig said, 'That is not our way, Neman. We will take our chances in space.'

Stung by the tone, Neman was angry in turn, 'Do you think we wanted this? You must believe us. Once our race has been established on the new planet . . . we, Kara, the other Darians will gladly die.'

A confused noise of shouting and running feet made an interruption. A Darian, blood streaming from a head wound, burst in through the hatch. 'Neman . . . the Survivors . . . they've broken in!'

To give him his due, Neman never hesitated. He ran to meet the enemy with the two Darians behind him.

Helena was stirring. Her eyes were open. Koenig knew he should be where the action was, but went to her, held her tightly for human comfort, said, 'Helena. Relax. It's all right. We'll have you out of here in no time at all.'

She was seeing him in double vision and his voice was coming from a long way off, but the message was received and understood. She said, 'John!' in a whisper and her eyes closed again.

Remembering his own experience under a Darian drug, he reckoned she would be okay the next time round. He said, 'Stay with her, Victor,' and went out, followed by Kara.

The noise of battle had rolled into the Command Centre and when he reached the open hatch Koenig could see it was only a matter of time before the surviving Darians were overwhelmed.

Neman had lost his blaster and was struggling chest to chest with a wild, half-naked Survivor. Over the man's shoulder he saw that Hadin had gone to the gene bank and had plucked out the flat, oblong casket that held the glowing nucleus. In a surge of mad strength, the Darian Commander threw his opponent aside and forged through the press to save the most precious item on his world.

He was almost there, hands stretched out to grab for it when Hadin swung round, sensing danger. One way was as good as another to kill a pig. Hadin slammed the gene bank in a crashing blow on the crown of Neman's head. It shattered.

Neman's scream was not to recognise his diamond moment of death, but the despair of one knowing that the long years of guardianship had come to nothing and all he had done had been lost in a moment of time.

Neman fell, dead, drenched by the viscous fluid in the container, wreathed by the blackened and dying strands of the Double Helix.

Hadin saw the face. All his life it had been the picture of a god. Awed and terrified he said, 'Neman!'

Other Survivors took up the cry. There was a rush for out. Alan Carter had to beat a path through the tide. He saw Koenig and shouted 'Commander!'

Koenig's voice stopped the rout, 'Wait!'

There was a pause, Koenig spoke into a sudden silence. 'Listen. You can't run from each other any more. If you people are to have any chance at all, you must come together. You must help each other.'

Kara was kneeling beside her leader. Her face was a tragic mask. She said bitterly, 'What future do we have now?'

Pointing to the Survivors, Koenig said, 'These people are your future. You have the knowledge. Use it well. Re-educate them. Prepare them so that their descendants will complete the voyage. There will be time for us to help you to re-establish the food chain. The rest is up to you. Both parties of Darians.'

Hadin looked at Kara and their eyes held for a long beat. There was a lot to understand, but Hadin was nobody's fool. He was catching on. His old authoritative bearing was back. There would be immense problems, but maybe there was a better future for his people. He strode forward and lifted Kara to her feet.

'Is it true? Is it possible as the stranger says?'

Koenig left them to it. He signalled to the Alphans. Nobody attempted to stop them as they went out. In the transplant room, he picked Helena from her bed and carried her across his arms on the long trek to the Eagle.

In Main Mission on Moonbase Alpha, Sandra Benes who had refused all offers of a relief operator was first to see the pod on the alien spacer disgorge Eagle One. She called, 'I have them! They're coming out!'

It was crystal clear on the big screen. Eagle One veered away from the vast ship and picked up a course for home. Kano called, 'Main Mission to Eagle One. Come in, Eagle One. Nice to see you . . . what happened?'

Alan Carter flipped a switch, 'Eagle One to Main Mission. Even nicer to hear you. Ask me again when you have a spare hour. I'll tell you sometime.'

In the co-pilot seat, Koenig said, 'We can get in one trip before *Daria* goes out of range. As fast as you like, Alan. I'll leave it to you.'

He thumped the release stud of his harness. By this time Helena would be sitting up and taking notice. He wanted to be there. But Carter had a question that was bugging him, 'Commander. If the same happened on Alpha would you have chosen differently?'

It had been in Koenig's mind also and it was difficult to give an honest answer. He played for time, 'Let's hope I never have to make that kind of choice.'

In the rumble, Helena was sitting beside Bergman, eyes closed, looking pale and exhausted. Bergman moved over and Koenig took his place. He lifted her hand from the squab and put it to his mouth.

She opened her eyes and looked at him. 'We wouldn't have done that would we, John?'

'Who knows what anybody will do when they're driven by a sense of mission. I'd like to think we wouldn't do it for personal survival.'

'It's better for us to be on our own search.'

'I'd agree to that.'

CHAPTER SIX

Even the farthest reaching probes could no longer search out *Daria* from the interstellar wastes and bring her to the big screen. The Moon fled on, hurled ever deeper into the unknown. Koenig debated whether or not he should have pushed the idea of joining the Darians. But he told himself it was water under the bridge. He ought to clear the matter out of his head. Junk it. The past was dead.

But the past was raising more than one spectre and he reckoned, irritably, it must be a sign of age. In some way, he had a feeling that the past was not finished with them and every day that went by saw the impression gaining strength.

He found he was spending more time in the Technical Section, watching Victor Bergman's patient progress with his prototype cold engine and envied him the scientific single mindedness which could cut out all the surroundings and concentrate on an idea.

Bergman said, 'The problem will be to find a practical, inexpensive fuel.'

'Like coal?'

'Coal could never be made over into a single crystal. Natural gas might serve. But as I see it, old fashioned petroleum has the edge. You'll have to find a planet with oil reserves.'

'There must be some.'

'Not to refine into gasoline you understand. We'd set it up for naphthalene.'

'Keep the moths out for a start!'

'You can smile, John, but that's the crystalline hydrocarbon I need. Cheap, clean, efficient. An industrial revolution without the smog.'

Koenig roamed around the workshop. When he returned to the bench he had a question that was so far off the topic that Bergman straightened up and looked at him. 'What's your view of past time?'

Victor Bergman wiped his hands on a wad of tissue. He could see it was important to his friend. 'I thought you had something on your mind. Why do you ask?'

'Helena has Calder under observation.'

'Jim Calder?'

'The same. He's under stress. She's been digging back in old reports. Maybe that triggered it for me; but I feel that the past is suddenly very close.'

'The past is always with us in memory banks. Sometimes in more detail than we expect. I believe it has another real presence.

'In what sense?'

'Every scene, every act, every spoken word is a complex web of energy. Energy can neither be created nor destroyed. It goes on existing. I believe it is transmitted like a programme, as the ripples go on in a lake. It goes out beyond the gravisphere of Earth. Space is shot through with the drifting record of past time.'

'And with delicate enough receptors your *programmes* could be played back?'

'Why not?'

'When you've finished your engine you should work on it. You'd solve all the archaeologists' problems at one go.'

'It isn't as far fetched as you think.'

Others on Moonbase Alpha were finding the past had a living reality. Maybe the blankness of the future had turned their minds to something more positive. Helena Russell, in fact, had a starting point in the medical case she was treating, but her interest had quickened and she was going into it in more depth than was strictly due.

The work had spilled over from the medicentre and she was using free time in her own quarters to polish up a report which was taking off in her imagination like a novella. Surrounded by tapes from the archives and remembering vividly her own part in some of the events, she had a curious sense of reliving the period before the break, when the Moon was still on shuttle link with its Earth base and the Probeship Mission was priority one.

She was typing the record, using headed paper that fitted the events – WORLD SPACE COMMISSION; sub heading, MEDICAL AUTHORITY: CASE REPORT NO. ALPHA /11/11R/7763 CAPTAIN CALDER (JIM).

Where it would go when she had finished it was anybody's guess. But part of the reason she gave to herself for doing it, was that she felt she owed it to Koenig to try to understand Calder. Koenig and Calder had been the leading figures in the Ultra Probe Mission which had been to make a manned landing on the new planet Ultra that Victor Bergman had discovered beyond the then known limits of Earth's solar system. When the mission had become an impossibility Calder had seemed to fall into apathy. Although he and Koenig had been close and were still friends, Calder was now operating as one of Alan Carter's Eagle Captains and tended to keep out of sight, taking a solitary line.

She read through her preamble. '*It was the 877th day since our Moon . . . left Earth. We were between galaxies, drifting through empty space, when Jim Calder began to believe he was closing a second time with his terrible adversary . . .*'

Frowning, she tapped the sleek hood of her silent keyboard. It was not her usual style at all. She debated whether or not to begin again.

The object of the exercise, Jim Calder, was sleeping fitfully in his own quarters. He had refused to stay in the medicentre and Helena had reluctantly agreed to his discharge.

He was Koenig's age and had some of the same qualities. Tall and massively built, he looked the rugged, outdoor type who would be most content leading an expedition over difficult country in the early days of Empire. For him, the unnatural confinement of Moonbase Alpha had been irksome and almost impossible to come to terms with.

He was reflecting tension in his sleep. Hands clenching and unclenching, face contorted with the struggle that was going on in his mind, he was close to some nightmare confrontation.

There was a sighing in the room, an infinitely distant clash of discordant electronic sounds, a crackling intake of breath like a wind fanning flames in dry scrub.

Suddenly Calder sat bolt upright, sweat in glistening beads on his forehead. His life was under threat and he had to move. Ducking suddenly and rolling out of bed, he was on his feet standing legs apart, looking around for cover. There was nowhere safe. He gave ground, weaving and feinting, until he was brought up by the bulkhead at his back. Palms flat on the fluted cladding, he traversed left until his searching hand hit the haft of a tomahawk in his collection of early hunting weapons.

It made all the difference to his mental set. From being a naked ape, he had graduated to *homo habilis* and could face his adversary with a weapon in his fist. Some of the terror went from his face. His moves were concentrated and definite as he dodged and weaved looking for an opening. Despite the danger, he looked more relaxed, even as though there was some satisfaction in fighting it out.

Calder dropped on one knee, paused, gathered himself and was in with a hoarse shout for a strike. The tomahawk wheeled in a glittering arc and thudded home on the console of the communications post. The noises in his head zeroed. Running with sweat and trembling from released tension, Calder stood staring at the quivering axe.

A call from the duty medico had taken Helena Russell to the Medical Centre and she was in time to catch the computer print out. Calder's monitors had peaked. She shoved down a call button on the communications post and heard the repeat of its call signal in Calder's room.

He backed away. For his money it was dead, but would not lie down. The call came again. He had reached his bed and picked up his comlock from the bedside table.

Helena's face in miniature appeared on the small screen.

'Calder? Are you all right?'

With an effort of will, he tried to steady his voice, but was only partly successful. 'Yes . . . yes . . . I'm fine now. Thank you, doctor.'

There was a stiffness in the dialogue that stemmed from more than the doctor-patient situation. Helena knew he did not like her and the feeling was mutual. Maybe she was resenting the special place he had in Koenig's friendship. She worked at it to keep her voice soothing, 'You had me worried. Computer raised the alarm. Your pulse and metabolic rate peaked into the red.'

'It was a dream. Some kind of nightmare. Nothing for you to bother about, doctor.'

'A traumatic experience?'

'No. An absurdity. Nothing. Really, nothing.'

'Then I hope you'll sleep more peacefully.

'Thank you. Good night.'

It was clear he wanted her to sign off. Thoughtfully, she stubbed the button and the screen blanked. Calder walked slowly to his direct vision port and looked out at the starmap. It was the same and not the same like a wave of the sea.

A jarring electronic discord made him wince. Some of the

fear came back to his face. He looked round his room as though he was seeing it for the last time and used his comlock to open the hatch. Outside, the corridor was at half light in the routine simulation for night on Moonbase Alpha. He padded out and closed the hatch behind him.

In Main Mission, John Koenig was filling a part of the night watch by playing chess with Kano, an exercise that most Alphans avoided, because it was depressing.

Running true to form, Kano said, 'Check.'

'You've been playing Computer all day.'

'I was hoping for a real game, Commander. I beat Computer every time.'

'You programme it.'

'True. But I didn't programme you.'

Computer buzzed urgently and Kano stretched across, 'Computer is protesting at the insult.' As he tore off the read out, he looked puzzled. 'Commander, this is for you. Jim Calder has entered the restricted area on launch pad four. He is not on duty.'

Koenig's reaction was instantaneous. Comlock whipped from his belt, he called, 'Jim?'

Calder had reached an outlet port marked EMBARKATION POINT and Koenig's voice spoke to him out of the open comlock in his hand. He looked down at it and again at the illuminated sign. The voice was more urgent. 'Jim? What goes on? Answer me.'

Calder ignored it. Koenig was on his feet, a worried man. He was half way to Main Mission's hatch as he called over his shoulder, 'Kano, cancel his comlock.'

It was done before Koenig was two strides on his journey and Calder's slight hesitation had cost him the initiative. He flashed his comlock at the exit door and there was no joy. He looked at it incredulously and then thumped it with his free hand. There was still no action.

Alan Carter, checking round his section, appeared and the sight of Calder in his pyjama slacks was novel enough to raise a grin. It was difficult for him having Calder in his section. The man had been high in the station hierarchy, but he could not say there had been any resentment and they got along well enough. He always tried to avoid any situation where it might be thought he was pulling rank on the senior man. He kept the tone easy, 'Jim? What brings you out of your trundle bed?'

There was no answer. Without looking at him directly, Calder moved close. Carter tried again, still keeping it light, 'What's the problem, Jim? Can't sleep? I've checked the doors and put the cat out.'

Calder had shifted his comlock to his left hand and his right swept across in a blow to the side of Carter's neck that left him out cold on his feet with the smile fixed like a mask. Before he had reached the deck, Calder had snatched his comlock and was using it to open the door.

It was the outlet for the stand-by Eagle and a boarding tube was waiting to carry the duty crew. Without a backward look, Calder went forward, shoving down activating studs with casual precision as though it was a routine mission. Now he was calm and purposeful, doing a job he knew. The tube accelerated away, homed on the Eagle's main hatch and he was on board.

Efficient and professional, he sealed the hatch, raced through to the Command Module and flipped the master lever from Automatic to Manual. Now the ship was his and Main Mission had no power to override his operating console. Meticulously, he began the sequence of pre lift off procedures.

Koenig had reached Carter and knelt beside him. His breathing was regular. He would be okay in the fullness of time. Calder's discarded comlock explained a lot. He called Main Mission. 'Kano. Jim Calder's gone through to the stand-by Eagle. He's using Carter's comlock. Stop him.'

'No good, Commander. Eagle is on manual control. Computer can do nothing.'

Koenig raced for the hatch, thumbed down the stud on his comlock and met another snag. A warning pinger sounded out and the illuminated legend changed its message, NO ACCESS. COUNTING DOWN.

Calculations raced through Koenig's head. It would be neat, but he reckoned there was a small margin. He used his Command channel for a direct link and called, 'Computer. This is a command order. Cancel safety regulations on launch pad four and give me access.'

The boarding tube clunked home on station. Koenig was aboard and shuttling out to the Eagle. Calder saw the action on his screen and glanced at the digital count down. It stood at ten seconds and flipped to nine. Red alerts flashed on the console. Kano could not control the manual system, but he could still signal and ABORT LIFT OFF glowed across the screen.

Coldly and deliberately, Calder hit the ignition button.

Eagle Four's motors blasted as Koenig's boarding tube hit the hatch coamings. He was two seconds waiting for the all clear. As the panel came alive with AIR LOCK SEALED, he directed his comlock at the hatch and went through at a run.

Fail safe mechanisms were beating Calder. With the hatch open, even manual switchgear had gone definitively to Non Op. The control spread was a barrage of red tell-tales. Jaw set hard, he thumped the release stud on his harness and heaved himself out of his bucket seat. He was coming through the connecting hatch to the passenger module and his hands were reaching up to the roof rack for a stun gun as Koenig hurled himself down the aisle.

It was Koenig's hand that closed on the first butt and the muzzle came into aim at point blank range less than half a metre off.

Calder went still. He had a gun, but he had to move to use it. Eyes fixed on Koenig, he said, 'Let me go, John.'

They had known each other too long and too well for any hatred. It was a straight issue. He would go if he could and Koenig would stop him if he could. Calder had to try. The hand holding the gun whipped down from the rack.

Koenig fired on reflex. Calder had no shade of a chance. He dropped face down on the deck.

Helena Russell was partly blaming herself. She believed she should have taken Calder into her medicentre earlier. It was no help to know that she had been partly influenced by Koenig's clear desire to play down any suggestion that there was a serious medical problem for his friend. The friendship, anyway, irritated her. It was a male club affair that excluded her and she felt it diminished her relationship with Koenig. There was also the plain, professional opinion that Calder was unstable and she couldn't begin to understand why Koenig would not accept it.

With Bob Mathias, she ran a full battery of diagnostic checks on the unconscious man, glad to have the opportunity to do it without his active resistance or Koenig's interference.

She was not wildly pleased when Koenig came in at the

tail end, obviously anxious and feeling bad about having to turn a stun gun on a long time comrade. It would be better to say what she had to say if they were alone. She said, 'Thanks Bob. That wraps it up. I can take it on from there. It's my watch. You can catch up on some sleep.'

Not deceived, Mathias grinned at Koenig. 'All right, doctor. I'll turn in then. Good night. Good night, Commander.'

Koenig nodded. He walked over to the patient's bed side and looked at the monitors. Life signs were weak but regular.

Helena joined him and anticipated his question as though she wanted the initiative to be on the medical side, 'As well as can be expected after a point blank stun.'

Koenig's sudden wince gave her no pleasure. She hated to hurt him. But his expression, as he looked at the sleeping man, strengthened her resolve to have it out. She believed he valued Calder too highly.

'I've been expecting something like this.'

He would not be drawn and she went on, 'He's *unstable*, John.'

This time she got a response. 'He's an individualist.'

'I'll never understand your admiration for him.'

It was an invitation for a confidential report, but it didn't work. Koenig said, 'Spoken like a true medico. You Doctors naturally resent those who don't need you.'

Taken in the context that Calder was unconscious and dependent on the hook up to life support systems, this seemed to her the nearest thing to nonsense she had ever heard from him. Partly on a professional basis and partly from personal pique at not being able to get through his pigheadedness, she took it further, 'John, I can read the signs. He's a text book case. He's a suppressed hysteric. Where do you think he was trying to get to out there – in his pyjama pants? We're nowhere. Three months Eagle travel to the fringe of the nearest star system. He didn't even pack a toothbrush.'

Koenig ignored the jibe and continued to look at the unconscious man. Driven to it she said flatly, 'You've gone out on a limb for him. You kept him here when he should have been grounded. You've done too much. Your image of him doesn't square with the medical record.'

At last Koenig looked at her and it was a bleak, challenging stare. 'You didn't know him before the Ultra Probe was launched.'

'That's true, but I know him now and I'm being *objective*.'

'Meaning that I'm not. A man doesn't change all that much. He was probably the world's best all round athlete. Arguably, the best poet of his generation; without question, he was the best astronaut to leave space base. He was one of the very few who excel both mentally and physically.'

'I *have* read his file.'

Koenig ignored the terse comment. He went on, 'But something happened out there, beyond Ultra – something neither you nor I can understand. And *he* can't understand it either. It's haunted him. It's destroying him. He does his job as an Eagle pilot, because he can do that with a tenth of the knowledge and the talent he has. I've no complaints. But I know him as he really is and he rates all the breaks I can give him.'

Helena Russell hesitated. There was more on her side of the argument and she was gauging whether or not this was the time to come clean. She said slowly, 'I know the Ultra Probe meant a lot to you, John. But the success of the mission was *vital* to Calder. He can't take failure. For that reason alone, you would've been the better Commander of the Probe. Personal identification with a project at an extreme level is bad for clear judgement. You would have kept a better balance.'

'Leave me out of it. Stick to Calder.'

'Very well. I'd say he made a disastrous mistake in that Probeship. As the acknowledged ace and wonder man, he just couldn't bring himself to admit it.'

Koenig glared at her. 'That's just not Calder. You've got it all wrong.'

'He may believe he's infallible and that's no good sign for mental health, but we don't have to go along with it.'

'Nothing was proved at the investigation.'

This time, there was the suspicion of a defensive note in Koenig's voice. He could not reconcile anything she said with his belief in Calder, but he also believed she was sincere. She recognised that she could take the case no further without a confession which would make her unpopular, but honesty demanded it. She walked away from Koenig to her desk. From there, it was an official communiqué. 'John. At the time it all happened, I was one of the medical team that examined Calder. My report on the areas I was given to investigate, reinforced the case against him.'

There was no doubt that it came as a shock to Koenig. He

had been close to Calder. He was close to Helena. It took some adjustment to see that two parts of his own personal fabric could be opposed to each other. Maybe he would come round to the idea, but the time was not yet. All he could understand was that she had been responsible for the official destruction of his friend's reputation.

There was no improvement when she went on, 'I presented the facts as I saw them.'

Angrily, he snapped, 'There *were* no facts.'

She tried to ignore the slur on her professionalism. Keeping her voice steady, she put it on the line. 'John, he *is* unstable. He's a threat to the safety of Alpha.'

Koenig's voice was a shout. 'Maybe you're saying I should have used the laser instead of the stun?'

Her resolution to keep it official took a knock. She had not been at the receiving end of his anger before. She moved towards him with some half formed intention to get things back on a personal level, where they could look at the problem from the same side of the fence. 'John . . .'

The appeal was lost. He was on his way to the hatch. As a parting shot over his shoulder he said, 'Why not write another report to the Space Commission?'

For her money it was all very unfair and, for that matter, unlike Koenig. Still, there was always work, the great therapy. She checked Calder's monitors. There was no change. Physically, he would be all right. Another hour and he would be back on circuit. She wished she could understand him better for Koenig's sake. But in spite of the sneers, facts were facts and the interpretation had been as honest and objective as she could make it.

She stood at a direct vision port, looking out over the bleak moonscape to the starmap. Nothing changed and yet there was a subtle pervasive feeling of strangeness in the quiet ward. Maybe it was heightened by the emotional tension of the conflict with Koenig? The past seemed very vivid and real. She returned to her desk and picked up Calder's file. She could at least clear her mind by continuing the account she had begun.

Calder stirred uneasily and she pulled a low chair to the side of his bed and sat with the file on her knee. She would make notes and type it up later.

As she leaned back against the upholstery, suddenly conscious that she was tired, her head was directly below the cluster of cables that hooked Calder to the monitor spread. She felt a slight tingling over her scalp and shivered. The old saying 'Somebody walking over my grave' went through her mind.

Then the familiar outlines of the medicentre slipped out of focus and she was the unseen witness of a different time and a different place . . .

CHAPTER SEVEN

Helena Russell could see the Technical Section, crystal clear as though she was present in it and from the NASA picture of Earth on the TV screen and the space news signature jingle, she knew the date was way back. The legend SPACE NEWS faded and an announcer was cued in, 'Space News, dateline nine, three ninety-six, brought to you from Houston, planet Earth...'

Calder and John Koenig, both wearing the uniform of Alpha's reconnaissance section were deep in concentration on detailed plans of the Ultra Probeship and photographs and constructional drawings were pinned up on every vertical surface. Victor Bergman was there, at his own desk sorting through a stack of data sheets and computer read-outs.

The two astronauts were too engrossed to take in the news flash, but Bergman paused in his work and watched the screen.

As a backdrop to the announcer's bland head, there was now a picture of the probeship herself, docked on a limb of the space station in orbit around the Moon.

The announcer went on, 'The Ultra Probe. Speculation mounts on who will command the ship. Anton Gorski, Commander of Moonbase Alpha, is expected to be in a position to reveal the name at the end of this week...'

It was nothing fresh to Bergman. He had all the imponderables he could handle. He left his desk and flipped a switch to cut the transmission. The onset of silence reached the other two and they looked up.

Bergman said, 'They're still going on about who's to take the Ultra Probe. One thing's for sure, we need a decision. You know you both can't go.'

It earned him a blank look as though it was, in fact, a thing they did not know and he went on, 'Well, you must see someone's got to mastermind the whole operation from here. You'd agree, I take it, that you can't leave it to Gorski?'

There was a hard core of truth in that one and they looked at each other and shrugged. Koenig said: 'So?'

Scientific to his finger tips, Bergman brought a coin out of his pocket and threw it to Koenig.

Koenig fielded neatly, a tribute to his reaction time and looked at Calder, 'Okay to you, Jim? Winner takes the ship, loser tells the Old Man.'

He pitched the coin across the table and called. Calder trapped it on the back of his hand. There was a slight hesitation and Helena wondered how he would react if he was loser. But then he was thrusting it forward for Koenig and Bergman to see and his face was split in a delighted grin.

He said, 'At least the gods of chance know who's the better astronaut.'

Generous though disappointed, Koenig made it easy by keeping a light tone, 'Nonsense, they know where the best brains of this operation need to be. That's here on Alpha ... All the same, I could wish they were less knowledgeable.'

Bergman looked from one to the other, grave and unsmiling. It was a decision — which was good; but whether it was the right decision, he could not be sure. He said, 'I take it that's agreed, then?'

The scene changed, dissolved and reformed. Helena recognised Alphans she had not seen since the Moon went off on its solitary junket. There was a crowd, milling around the entrance to the air lock at the embarkation point for the space station. It was a farewell ceremony for the Probeship crew. Koenig and Bergman were in the forefront shaking hands with the four astronauts.

Calder was full of confidence. Photogenic and tough, he was everyman's image of a spacefarer. Beside him were Doctor Darwin King and Professor Juliet Mackie. Slightly to one side, but watching her captain with clear admiration was the trim figure of Doctor Olga Vishenskya.

Helena Russell was making notes on her pad. She accepted what she saw, as if it was a reconstruction in her mind's eye. *Launch date for the Ultra Probe was the sixth of June, ninety-six. Commander was Captain Jim Calder. Astrophysicist and Number Two was Doctor Darwin King. Radiation expert was Professor Juliet Mackie and Doctor Olga Vishenskya was responsible for medical, dietary and psychological well-being of the team. They were shuttled to the interplanetary space station where the Ultra Probeship was docked.*

She could see it as if the big screen in Main Mission had

set it up. The Eagle arrowed away for the short crossing and homed on a docking collar in the great wheel.

Calder and his crew had a gauntlet of well wishers to run as the station personnel turned out to see them through to the hatch of the Probeship. Then they were inside and the hatch was slicing shut with a definitive click.

Wasting no time, Calder strode through to the Command Module, leaving the other three in the spacious Ward Room. It was a rest area and a workshop both, stacked with sophisticated hardware and giving access to four cubicle cabin areas which would give each one a private base for the long star trek.

Once aboard they were all anxious to be away and they strapped into acceleration couches for the blast off. King checked around and called on his intercom, 'Ready when you are, Jim.'

Helena recorded it meticulously, *'Embarkation and countdown proceeded without a hitch. Launch took place at twelve hundred hours. Exactly on schedule.'*

Once again, she saw the gleaming spacer jack itself into the starmap and join the myriad wheeling stars. She had a sudden sympathy with Koenig and Calder and the way they had thought about the mission. 'The last Knight of Europe takes weapons from the wall.' It was in the great romantic tradition, a gesture against the blank, vastness of the cosmos.

The Probeship hurled itself on like a flung spear. Watches changed. Calder and King alternated in the command slot. The crew settled to their routine.

Helena was recording again, unaware that there was anything strange about her dual role. *'So the longest ever manned space flight began. It continued through eight months of uneventful routine, speeding like a shuttle on the thread spun by its computers and watched and checked by the support team on Moonbase Alpha. Nothing disturbed the measured pace of the voyage as the Probeship ate up distance beyond comprehension. No malfunction broke the monotony. Navigation was faultless.'*

Helena was conscious that Calder was stirring uneasily. She put a hand on his shoulder and he went still; but the narrow hospital cot wavered and merged into something else. She was sitting with him in the command module of the Probeship and, plate sized in the direct vision port, she saw what he was seeing. Dark, mysterious and beautiful, the planet Ultra was dead ahead, precisely where Bergman had predicted it would be.

She could sense Calder's emotion and knew that here at least there was no personal vainglory in it. He was proud to be representing Earth's technological triumph, but he was rating himself as an agent and not the kingpin on which the enterprise revolved. There was another human emotion also to be counted. Olga Vishenskya, moving like a dancer, came in through the hatch with a cup of coffee for the top hand.

She said, 'The closer we get, the more beautiful it is.'

Calder took the cup and touched her fingers. There was clearly a special bond between them. He said, 'Thanks, Olga. What does Computer have to say?'

'Still mulling it over. But gravity, radiation, atmosphere – all look hopeful.'

'Mankind could use a fresh start. If we're ready for it.'

Darwin King ducked through the hatch and settled into the co-pilot seat. Olga went back to the work room.

Helena recorded, *'For days excitement mounted as progressive readings confirmed the planet's condition was similar to Earth's. Plans were made for a manned landing. Then for the first time, as the Probeship moved behind Ultra, all contact was temporarily lost with Moonbase Alpha. The landing was never made. The only record of what happened was subsequently given by Calder himself.'*

She had read the transcript and she had not been able to judge what was true and what was false. It had looked like a classic case of self-justification. Or it had been something dredged up from the unconscious mind to symbolise a man's internal battle with the dark forces of his own nature.

Now she was getting it first hand from the command module of the Probeship . . .

The four astronauts were working at fever pitch, checking, analysing, searching for an optimum site to put down an excursion module. They were hardly aware that they were out of contact with Moonbase Alpha.

The Probeship curved in a long arc for a proving orbit. Alerted by pin point traces on his radar scan, Calder tuned for magnification and called through the hatch, 'Darwin, could you give me an opinion here, please.'

There was something in the tone that brought Darwin King through the hatch at a run. The scan made no kind of sense. A puzzled man, he looked at Calder, 'Metallic?'

'You tell me. Small and stationary for sure.'

King took readings, 'Orbital reference one zero nine.'

'Beam scanners, sensors, the whole shooting match on one zero nine. We're going to take a look.'

There was the briefest hesitation from Darwin King, lost on Calder, who was totally concentrated on bringing the Probeship to a new course. Sensitive to all the nuances of the situation, the observer from future time knew what he was thinking. They were out of touch with Moonbase Alpha. Any deviation ought to be cleared with control or at least reported. But it was momentary. All tracking gear swung from Ultra to the new target. The Probeship turned and headed off.

Helena Russell saw it through Calder's eyes as the Probeship halved and quartered the distance. It was a graveyard of space junk, a small Sargasso Sea of lifeless spacers, drifting in a slow spin as though caught in a timeless eddy of interstellar forces. There was no uniformity. They were not from one place or one time. Random chance had brought the collection to the fringes of Ultra's gravisphere.

The watchers on the Probeship stared out from direct vision ports in silent amazement. They had netted a technological museum. The implications for research into other spacefaring civilisations were enormous.

Olga Vishenskya breathed, 'Fantastic!'

Sharing the same view port, Juliet Mackie asked, 'Where have they come from? For that matter, what are they doing here?'

Darwin King rechecked the sensors.

'Negative. No sign of life from any one of them.'

Olga said, 'Can they really be empty?'

There was an ominous, brooding quality about the silent ships. Trying to lighten it, Juliet said, 'There's a conference on. A space nation conference. This is the vehicle park.'

Calder took her literally. 'Where's the conference then? Not on Ultra. We have no life signs from Ultra.'

He was taking the Probeship in. Thrust cut back, they were sliding between the stationary spacers, the only purposeful item in the field. He said, 'There's got to be someone around. Check with computer, Darwin. And Juliet, put a booster on every band in the life spectrum. Give me a little information.'

Olga remained with him in the command module. She said slowly, 'It's science fiction vindicated on a big scale. Victor Bergman'll have a field day.'

The Probeship was crossing the centre, dwarfed by a huge spacer almost all power pack with a proton drive dish at its stern. The crew module in the cone was tiny by comparison. Marvin King came through the hatch and Calder said, 'There are ships here that could make the dream of interstellar travel a reality. We could be liberated from our own solar system – from our own galaxy even.'

'All we need is an ancient mariner to show us how it works.'

'Still no signs of life?' There was an edge of disappointment in Calder's voice.

'Absolutely none. It's like a necropolis.'

'Well the tombs of the Pharaohs taught us all we know about Ancient Egypt – so let's see if we can break into this one.'

The Probeship was approaching a long wasp-waisted spacer with a green and yellow geometric emblem enamelled on the cone. Calder manoeuvred for a position above a series of plexiglass domes and said, 'I'll go in close. Darwin, you and Juliet can take a walk and see what you can find. Back them up, Olga.'

There was a flurry of activity as the three shrugged into space gear and sealed up. Calder sat alone in the command module, drumming his fingers on the console and staring out along the hump back of the spacer below him. It was a discovery that ranked with the mission to Ultra itself. He could imagine the impact in scientific circles when they released the data that could be gathered from any one of these ships.

King broke into his reverie, 'All set, Captain. Ready to de-pressurise.'

Calder flipped switches in a row. The air lock between his command module and the main cabin closed with a hiss. Using the intercom, he said, 'De-pressurising as of now. Maintaining normal gravity.'

There was a pause. Olga sat at her desk. Marvin King waited at the hatch with Juliet behind him. Calder's voice came again, 'Opening airlock.'

As the hatch began to slide open, Olga lifted a bulky thumb as a good luck gesture.

It was premature. Instead of the black night of space, the

open port was filled from edge to edge with a pulsating glob of flickering light. Writhing across it and already moving to probe into the cabin was a nest of living tentacles. Suction built to a violent storm and loose trash whipped away into the vibrant maw.

Olga's scream was lost in the outlandish electronic screech of a gale of fire sucking down an endless tunnel.

Darwin King was gripped and held. Arms outstretched, he tried to hang on to the hatch coaming. But he was wrenched away. Juliet's despairing cry, 'Close the hatch,' was seconds late to save him and Calder, hitting the cancelling stud, was, anyway, getting no joy. He called, 'I can't close it. It's jammed.'

'For God's sake close it.' Juliet's agonised plea tailed off in a scream as a shadowy tentacle searched her out.

The Probeship's power pack shrieked into overload and a rash of red warning lights glared from the console as the straining gear tried to close the hatch. But the phenomenal strength of the obscene arms kept it prised open. Calder was racing to climb into his space suit. Screams from Olga and Juliet lacerated his mind. There was a pause, a momentary lull in the electronic clamour and a panting silence. Darwin King's body, feather light, jetted from the open hatchway to roll like a thistledown ball to Juliet Mackie's feet.

Her renewed screams melded in a new surge of racket and a tentacle clamped itself round her waist.

Olga Vishenskya was crouched in the entrance of the hatch to the command module. Reaching overhead she grabbed two lasers from the rack and pitched one to Juliet. They fired through the open door into the burning throat. Noise notched up in an insane crescendo. Then Juliet Mackie was gone, hauled struggling and still firing her laser into the flaming orifice.

Olga's screams were hysterical and continuous. Calder heard it from his console and again blasting into his head as he slammed on his helmet and snapped down the seals. 'Help me, Jim! Help! Help!'

'I'm on my way. Hold on!'

There was another lull and Juliet Mackie's drained and lifeless husk was flung into the ward room. Olga was facing the closed door, beating on it with clenched gauntlets. 'Jim!'

A probing, dark rope hit her back. The raging noise increased again. A second tentacle reinforced the first and slid round her throat. When Calder had the hatch open, she was already a metre off as the arms retracted to pull her away.

Calder was in the hatch, striving to see past her, firing again and again at an amorphous black bulk that filled the main cabin. Then a pin point of light separated out and widened and opened like a flower in time lapse to show the brilliant burning maw of the monster.

One arm flung forward to shield his eyes from the glare, Calder fired until the charges ran out. He saw Olga dragged and thrust into the eager throat. Her dying scream was drowned out in the maniacal clatter.

It was no good. There was nothing he or anybody else could do. He backed away, stumbling through the hatch into his command module and shoved the stud to seal it off. The hatch was ten centimetres from a closure when a viridian probe, pitted with suckers and exuding a viscous slime thrust itself into the gap.

Ripping open the crash locker, Calder dumped out every kind of cutting gear and settled for a long shafted, woodman's axe. Suction was raising a gale wind through the crack and he had to hold himself to one side to operate at all.

Olga's body skidded over the deck and lodged on the outside of the half open hatch. He swung and struck at the writhing arm like a raving madman.

At first there was no visible progress. He was losing. The tentacle engorged and in its swelling shoved open the panel a few more centimetres. Calder spared a split second to turn up the valve on his oxygen supply and went to work again. He had seen a small break in the tissue. Two out of three, he was hitting the spot. The blade sank in. He wrenched it free and swept down for another blow with every atom of weight and strength he could bring to bear.

When it almost sheared through and the wounded limb whipped away, the hatch slammed shut. He leaned on the axe, weak and shaken, with sweat masking his face and misting his visor.

Driving himself to move, he staggered to the pilot seat and dropped into it. He pressed the stud to re-pressurise and watched the gauge in dull apathy until the indicator moved into the green quadrant. Then he unsealed his helmet with shaking fingers and lifted it off.

There was a wrenching and scrabbling at the hatch. The monster had not finished yet. Hands moving desperately slowly, he pressed a sequence of emergency keys on the console. A panel slid open revealing a switch and the words MODULE EJECTION.

As he shoved over the lever, the whole hatch structure was shuddering in its housing. Explosive bursts ran round the hull of the Probeship as retaining bolts were blown out. The small auxiliary motor fired. The command module separated itself from the rest of the ship, rolling like tumble weed through the graveyard.

For a space, Calder sat still, held by his harness, hardly realising that he was still drawing his ration of life's breath. Then he began to struggle with the controls. The module shuddered as he fired stabilisers. It was through the junkyard, off into eternity. He wiped his face, settled to work again, brought it round on a course that would orbit Ultra. He was, after all, a professional and he had a small viable ship. It was up to him to get back.

Calder had gone still again and seemed more relaxed. Helena Russell recorded, *'Despite his ordeal, Calder executed a brilliant manoeuvre, which used energy, gathered in a calculated orbit round Ultra, to fling him out on a course for Earth. He survived alone in his small capsule for over eight months.'*

There was some truth in Koenig's estimate that Calder was the outstanding astronaut of the age. She could feel the loneliness and despair of the survivor as the tiny speck fled on through the wastes of space. She could even see Calder, as he had appeared to himself, reflected in the glass of the ports, unshaven, hollow eyed, emaciated, eking out the meagre survival rations, working by manual computation, navigating by an amalgam of instinct and knowledge.

She set it down, *'Calder's module was eventually located by John Koenig and he was picked up and brought back to Alpha. His triumph was subdued, because he himself was on the point of death.'*

Now she was seeing the very moment of homecoming. It was the embarkation in reverse, with the whole base turning out to see him brought off the relief Eagle. Bob Mathias checked the stretcher party and Calder's thin face on the pillow could have been a death mask. Mathias said, 'Straight into the Intensive Care Unit.'

As the trolley rolled on, Koenig spoke to Mathias, 'Bob?'

'It's unbelievable that he's alive at all.'

'Has he a chance?'

'He has the courage.'

'That's for sure.'

Helena wrote, *'But as Calder began to recover his strength, the official attitude to him changed from congratulations to doubt. The story he told of his encounter with the monster was difficult to believe and the recorded data of the black box cast further doubt on his veracity. As a member of the Space Commission Medical Team, I was detailed to enquire into the mental state of the patient.'*

With a sense of déja vu, Helena saw herself with another white coated figure walking down a corridor in a base hospital at the Space Centre on Planet Earth. They turned off into a private room and Calder, sitting up in bed tracked them in over the top of a journal. He looked almost back to normal.

She saw herself being introduced. Her guide said, 'Captain Calder?'

'That same one.'

'This is Doctor Helena Russell – from Space Commission Medical Centre.'

Calder's smile had almost professional charm. He could have been an actor. 'Welcome, Doctor. I expect you've come to talk. Please. A chair for Doctor Russell. You have come to hear the story. You'd better be comfortable. It takes some time and with such a beautiful listener I shall be tempted to make it longer.'

'Thank you, Captain.'

'I'd say, "Call me Jim"; but in the circumstances you may not want to do that!'

There was something odd about that; but in the gestural fuss of settling her in a chair, it went past. She spoke to her colleague, 'Thank you.'

'A pleasure. I'll leave you to it.'

There was a silence. Helena, trying to minimise the professional status that had brought her there, settled herself like a regular bedside visitor and smiled at him in the interests of good *rapport*. But Calder was giving her a shrewd look and was still on his ironic tack, 'It depends, I suppose, on whether you've come to confirm a prejudice or listen with an open mind.'

She was not fully tuned in, 'I'm not sure that I know what you mean?'

'Come on, Doctor! They don't believe me. How can they? You see, the green eyed monster from outer space is as fixed a stereotype as in the picture books of childhood fantasy. Like Santa Claus. How can they possibly believe?'

'Wait a minute. You're way ahead of me. We seem to have started off on the wrong tack.'

'Sorry, Doctor. But you're not the first, though I'll concede you're the prettiest. I've been through this sequence a dozen times. The fact is, if a guy with a red coat and a white beard drove into town with reindeer and a sleigh and started handing out goodies, he'd be arrested on a corruption ticket. Or certified as insane. Kid's stuff. Unbelievable.'

Helena's laugh was genuine. He was a good talker with a nice, mocking style. But Calder added seriously, 'Now be an honest medico. That's what you're going to do with me and my monster. Right?'

'Who brought up the monster? I didn't mention it.'

'But that's what you wanted to talk about, isn't it?'

'I didn't have anything specially in mind. Certainly no prejudice. Open to anything. Santa Claus if he interests you.'

Calder was watching her, making judgements of his own and his suspicion took another turn, 'Just a diplomatic mission to establish good relations?'

'If you like.'

'If *you* like, Doctor. You're calling the shots. After all *you* came to see *me*. And a big improvement on any bunch of grapes or an Arum Lily. Maybe in a while we'd get around to my sex life? Restricted though it is, as of now.'

'Who knows? You seem pretty keen to talk on a fairly wide range of topics.'

Calder's eyes narrowed in earnest and he leaned towards her. 'Cards on the table, Doctor. I want to tell you that everything I put down in my report is the truth as I know it. Tentacles, blood suckers, fiery breath, warts and the whole goddam shooting match. The whole, slimy, fantastic story is *true*. No cover up to protect my reputation. No wandering of a sick mind bemused by solitary confinement and starvation. I'm absolutely certain of every detail I've put down and if the black box data conflicts with my telling of it, then the black box has it *wrong*.'

He was deadly serious and his eyes never wavered. Helena said mildly, 'Now that's a somewhat surprising statement for a rational man.'

He thumped the covers with a balled fist as a substitute, no doubt, for thumping conviction into his visitor. There was a sudden element of real anger in his voice, 'I am *not* a rational man.'

'Yet you claim belief?'

There was a change in Calder. He had gone pale and was breathing hard. His urbane manner was long gone. Speaking quickly and thumping the bed for emphasis, he said, 'I want all of you, Koenig, Bergman, Gorski and that fool Commissioner Dixon, every one of you to throw out the existing criteria by which you judge what is real. You've got to abandon reason. You have to *believe* that I, Jim Calder, athlete, poet and astronaut from Earth, have been out into the jungle behind Ultra and stood face to face with a dragon. I have fought it single handed and survived. *That's* what you've got to believe.'

Calder fell back on his pillows. Sweat was running down his face. A muscular tremor had started up and he shivered uncontrollably. His eyes were haunted, almost demented as he stared at Helena.

She was on her feet, ready to call the local staff. But the doctor who had brought her in had been watching on remote vision. He was already coming through the door with a hypo gun and made soothing noises as he took Calder's trembling arm.

'Easy, Captain. Easy now.'

Calder was not finished. With a sudden burst of fury, he swept the hypo gun away. His voice was an angry shout. 'Get that rubbish away from me!'

The hypo gun skidded over the polished floor. As the doctor went to retrieve it, Calder went quiet. Almost pathetically, he looked up at Helena. 'It's not too much to ask, Doctor? You'll understand.'

'I understand.'

Her touch seemed to soothe him and he closed his eyes. She signalled for the hypo gun and shot in a tranquillising charge.

Then she stood looking at his sleeping face. It was difficult, but he had presented her with a straight-forward clinical picture. He believed what he said. There was no doubt about that. But there could be no positive assurance that what he believed was fact. Only external, objective evidence could prove it one way or another.

She was still looking at Calder's sleeping face in her own medicentre and she was still sure that her report had been the only thing she could do at the time. It had triggered the detailed enquiry and now in her mind's eye she could see what neither she nor Calder could have seen as the faint residual traces of that time replayed themselves through Calder's sensitised receptors and passed by symbiosis to her own head.

On Moonbase Alpha Victor Bergman was examining the Probeship's Black Box when Koenig burst in on him full of indignation, 'Victor, there's going to be a full scale enquiry. Commissioner Dixon has ordered us back to Earth.'

Bergman looked up from his task. He seemed unsurprised. Koenig went on, 'The angle is that Jim bungled the decompression procedure, prematurely opened the air lock and killed the crew.'

Bergman looked at him calmly. 'If you want logic, I can only say that it would be a logical explanation.'

Koenig's shocked look prompted him to go on. 'You have to concede, John, that's easier to believe than a monster.'

'Victor, if the black box didn't record the monster, it could just conceivably be a life form that our instruments can't detect; maybe it jammed the black box. I know it's hard to take. But just because we haven't had experience of such a thing, it doesn't mean it can't exist. Where would science be on that tack?'

'We're not likely to know for sure unless we go back for a second look.'

'There's no doubt on that one. We *must* go back. Those spacers could save the Space Programme billions. And not just the money. Time. Hundreds of years of progress. We know Jim wasn't fantasising about them. The contacts are there – on record.'

'Contacts, John. That's all they are. There's no indication that they're spaceships.'

Koenig was nettled. 'Come on, Victor. You know Jim. Do we have to disbelieve everything he says?'

There was real sympathy in Bergman's voice as he said,

'He's virtually come back from the dead. It's natural for him to have nightmares. It would be unnatural if he didn't.'

'You're saying that he can't distinguish fact from fantasy in his own head. We can't let them dismiss it like that, Victor.'

Bergman sighed wearily. 'There's another factor, you know, John. Our probe was a failure from the politicians' point of view. Someone's head has to roll.'

'So they want a scapegoat and they've picked Jim?'

'While the balance of his mind is disturbed and I have to say he's not giving his friends much help.'

'His mind's far from disturbed. At least not in the way they think.'

'Unfortunately, Commissioner Dixon will have to rule on that and he's the last one to understand Jim Calder.'

The truth of Bergman's judgement was obvious when they were assembled in Dixon's office in the Space Commission zigurrat. He was the last man to see eye to eye with a romantic adventurer. Smooth and polished and adept at political double talk, he had one foot in the space enterprise and one in the corridors of power. To be fair, he had the job of squeezing funds out of the appropriations committee and many a man would have got less. But finance was clearly on his mind as he bustled importantly to his desk and waved to them to be seated. His manner was professionally genial and frank.

'Gentleman, there's nothing like the failure of a mission for giving the backers cold feet. Money dries up faster than a desert in drought. I hope you've all got sound ideas for limiting the lean time.'

Koenig looked at Calder, who was sitting with his arms folded and his mouth set in an ironic twist. Bergman was composed and serious. Neither seemed ready to speak. He decided to open the account himself. 'There were successful aspects of the mission, Commissioner. It would help if we could concentrate public attention on the potential of planet Ultra. It was established that it has Earth-like qualities.'

Dixon listened, head slightly to one side as though all attention. 'That doesn't have the PR power of a thumping, dramatic failure – at tremendous cost.'

Still batting, Koenig said, 'Then we should be positive. Launch the second probe right away. With the knowledge we have its success is assured. Put our experience to good use and get back out there.'

Dixon's half smile never wavered, 'Before we get carried away by the future, Koenig . . .' his eyes flicked to Calder and then back, '. . . We must dispose of the past. I want to know what you really think happened out there.'

He widened his range of vision to include Bergman. Both hesitated. Calder was in with a rush, 'I'm the only one who can answer that, Commissioner.'

There was no move from the other two. Reluctantly, Dixon fixed on Calder, 'And?'

'Nothing fresh. It's all in my report which you've had.'

The PR mask slipped a little. Dixon sounded genuinely angry, 'The whole world's had your report. That's my problem.'

'It's also the truth.'

There was silence. Dixon recognised he was cast for examining magistrate and had little taste for it, usually he delegated the hatchet work. But he had to make progress. 'So you say. So you say, *repeatedly*. Another plausible interpretation of the few facts we have, is that you have put up an elaborate smoke screen as cover-up for an error of judgement you haven't the guts to admit. What would you say to that one?'

'That it isn't true.'

'And the *recorded* deaths by decompression?'

'The way the beast sucked the life out of them could possibly record that way on the log.'

'So it's your word against the flight box and I don't have to tell you that no technical investigator has ever faulted the record of that piece of equipment.'

He turned away abruptly and addressed the other two. 'I need to hear what you two have to say. Do you believe in monsters?'

The sneer in the tail did him no good, but they had to concede his right to ask.

Bergman looked unhappy, 'I believe that whatever happened affected Jim's mind in some way he doesn't recognise and we can't even guess at.'

'Koenig?'

'I'm inclined to believe in the existence of the spaceships. At least we have evidence for them.'

Dixon put his elbows on his desk top and rested his forehead on the tips of his fingers as though checking that the roof of his brain was not lifting off. He said slowly and clearly, 'We have a group of unidentified and unidentifiable blips recorded from the scanner. That's what we have. So far as I'm concerned, the vision of a spaceship graveyard is as much a product of a sick mind as a ghoulish monster. Let's keep with the facts.'

He lifted his head and stared hard and straight at Bergman, 'Tell me straight, Professor. What caused the interference on that tape?'

Bergman shifted uncomfortably, 'Impossible to say. It could be any one of . . .'

Dixon leaned forward and stubbed a finger at Calder, 'Could it have been done by Captain Calder?'

It was a question Victor Bergman would have liked to duck, but silence would be more damaging. He said slowly, 'Technically, Jim could have done it – but I don't know why he should.'

Dixon found no problem there, 'As a cover-up.'

Koenig came in hotly, 'Then why in god's name should he restart normal recording four minutes and forty-five seconds later?'

Deliberately obtuse Dixon said, 'Are you going to suggest the monster did it, Koenig?'

'It has to be considered as a possibility. In a negative sense. Whatever interference the alien force was exerting ceased to be exerted.'

The Commissioner's face was all mock sympathy, 'You surprise me, John.'

Koenig rejected the implied appeal.

'Commissioner, the decompression bit just doesn't hold water. If that's what happened, why didn't he simply re-close the air lock and re-pressurise. Why spend three minutes getting into a space suit?'

Bergman backed him, 'Also it has to be admitted that Jim's return to Alpha was a brilliant space manoeuvre. I put his chances of survival to computer. They were less than a million to one. I don't believe any man would deliberately put himself at that kind of risk just to save his reputation.'

Dixon sat back in his chair. It was clear to him he would get nowhere. He sounded disappointed.

'Quite obviously, you two are careless of your own reputations, but mine is bound up with the future of the Space Programme. You idealists have no regard for the political realities. I have to save what can be saved for the sake of future appropriations. And I'll do that. I'm afraid I shall have to be seen to discredit this whole adventure. Human error, we can reasonably accept. Imaginative crap won't go with the sort of committees I have to work through.'

Koenig interjected, 'But the planet? What about Ultra?'

The pained look from Dixon ought to have shut him up, but he went on urgently, 'Commissioner, we've had a lot of success with the Space Programme. We understand more and more of the physical nature of our solar system. We expect danger from radiation, neutron storms, black suns and the like, but we make a terrible mistake if we think we know it all. Investigation has to go on and in this project, the pathfinding has been done and brilliantly done.'

Climbing to his feet as a signal that he had heard all he was prepared to hear, Dixon put a cold edge on his voice for the crunch lines.

'Koenig, the reality of Space adventuring is that it is terribly *expensive*. The chances to do something big come infrequently – and only one at a time. This one has been loused up. I very much regret it; but I shall have to relieve you all of your posts.' Directly to Calder, he went on, 'You for some appropriate mental analysis, as a voluntary patient . . .'

Calder's mouth opened to voice an objection, but Dixon turned to the other two . . . 'And you two to remind you what it's like to have your feet on the ground.'

CHAPTER EIGHT

Helena Russell looked at the bulky file on her knee and at her pencilled notes. Around her, the medicentre was quiet and familiar. Calder was in peaceful and undisturbed sleep. She stood up, stretched, walked to a direct vision port and looked out at the velvet starmap.

She had the story outlined in her head as she would write it, vivid and detailed in some strange way. But she was no nearer the truth. She felt that she understood Koenig better and wished they had not parted in anger.

Instead of returning to the bedside, she went to her desk, took a fresh sheet of paper and brought the record up to date in her neat precise hand, *'By September 13th, 1999, the day the Moon blasted out of Earth's orbit, Dixon had been replaced and John Koenig was back on Alpha as Commander of the base. Victor Bergman was there as Scientific Adviser and Jim Calder was in the Eagle Section working as a pilot under Alan Carter's command.'*

She left the desk and ran a check on Calder's monitors. He was still unconscious, but life signs were stronger. It was strange. The record had come alive for her. She felt she had lived through the action from Calder's point of view. But how far was that due to the vivid prose in which he himself had written his reports? Thoughtfully, she returned to her desk and took up her pen, *'I was there too, as head of the Medical Section. Memory of the Probeship disaster was dimmed in our fight for survival until this lunatic attempt of Calder's to escape from Alpha. The old argument started again. Who could truly say what was fact and what was fiction?'*

A buzz from her comlock interrupted. Surprised to have such a late visitor, she shoved the pen in its clip and took her comlock from her belt. Koenig's face was in the palm of her hand.

'Helena, I want to apologise. Are you alone?'

That was an easy one to answer. Except for Calder, locked in his cloud of unknowing, she might have been the only sentient object in the vacant, interstellar spaces. Not letting him have it too smooth, she settled for the simple fact, 'Yes, I am.'

She put down the comlock and busied herself at the desk. She would be found unconcerned and professional. The hatch opened and Koenig was in, carrying a small hydroponic tank with a blue solution slopping around and a spectacular, blue hyacinth growing from a rooting basket.

Reservations melted. She was out of her swivel seat with a rush, her blonde hair surging as she ran to meet him. 'John!'

'What about that, then! I could never get cress to grow on blotting paper as a kid ... but, for you, the gods of horticulture, whoever they may be, took a hand. It's doing pretty well eh?'

She took it from him and it was suddenly awkward between them. Command trains its users to make snap decisions. He took it from her and put it carefully on the deck. Hands free, she could lace them behind his head. Her lips were soft as moss and a total encouragement to any amateur gardener.

Helena said, 'But where did you get it?'

'Must have been left behind by my predecessor, Commander Gorski. I found this pack in a locker. It looked as though it had growing potential, so I thought I'd give it a go ...'

'John, it's a wonderful present. Thank you!'

Honesty drove him to admit, 'I ... er ... did get a little advice from the boffins in hydroponics. But I can claim resolution and a sense of purpose. Anyway, sorry for chewing your head off. It's a beautiful head. How's the patient?'

She could have done without the switch, but he had paid his dues for any information that was going. She picked up her hyacinth and carried it carefully to her desk, 'No change, John. He's not giving me much help.'

'What baffles me is why he should crack now. It's years since Ultra. Why should he break now?'

'He'll never get over it. That's why I thought Alpha would be better off without him.'

It was an invitation for him to leave his entrenched position and come some way to common ground. Support for it came from an unexpected quarter. Calder himself said, 'Perhaps she's right, John.'

Guilt apart, Helena Russell was the more surprised of the two. Calder had struggled to raise himself to his elbows and she fairly ran to the monitors.

Koenig went to the man and put an arm round his shoulders, 'Steady now, Jim. Take it easy.'

Satisfied that he was not registering any dangerous surge on the monitors, Helena joined Koenig and nodded in response to his unspoken question.

Koenig said, 'Where were you trying to go, Jim? It's an empty quarter. There's nothing in any direction you could reach.'

Calder shuddered. His nightmare was still vivid. 'I felt it . . . I felt there was something . . . near.'

'What was it, Jim?'

Calder's eyes were not seeing them. He was staring at something in the depths of his own mind. Helena prompted him, 'The nightmare . . .' he turned his head to look at her and she went on, 'At 0347 last night. Medical Computer raised the alarm.'

'Yes. It was a dream. Just a dream. It was nothing.'

Koenig lowered him to his pillow. 'Some dream. Do you know what we found? There was that showpiece tomahawk buried in the Communications Post in your quarters.'

Calder made no reply, but his quick look at Koenig showed that he was very much aware of what was implied.

'Was it the monster, Jim?'

Calder grabbed the top bar of his hospital bed and heaved himself into a sitting position. Except that he looked tense, he was back to normal. He said, 'I don't understand it. I'd put that episode out of my mind. At least, it was under control. I haven't had a nightmare like that in years.'

'Then why now? And what did you aim to do about it? In the Eagle? Were you trying to get away from it?'

The answer was unexpected. Calder was surface calm. He looked every centimetre a rational man. The impression was that he knew what he had to do, though the mission was infinitely dangerous. Hard voiced, he said, 'I was going to face it.'

Helena looked at Koenig. He was finding it no easier than she was to make any sense out of it. A buzz from the Communications Post broke the impasse. Paul Morrow was on the screen, 'Commander, we have a contact. Could you come to Main Mission please?'

Koenig said, 'Check. Be with you, Paul.'

The screen blanked and Koenig turned to Helena, 'Take care of him, Helena. I'll be right back.'

Calder watched him go. There was a kind of serenity and assurance about him, which was in contrast to his behaviour over the last days. Watching him, Helena would have said that he had come together in his mind as though at last he knew for a truth he would be vindicated.

Every operator in Main Mission was watching the big screen. Victor Bergman saw Koenig come through the hatch and called 'John, something quite extraordinary...'

It needed no footnote. It was all there. Sandra Benes had it tuned up in a spectacular display. They were looking at a spaceship graveyard, a clearing in the forest where elephants came to die. Prominent in the foreground was an immense battle cruiser of utterly alien technology.

Alan Carter said, 'It's a kind of space motor show. No models giving a winsome writhe on the hoods though.'

Koenig ignored it. Eyes fixed on the screen, he said quietly, 'Well, Victor?'

Bergman understood. 'All right, John. It's the same kind of thing that Calder described from the far side of Ultra.'

Koenig turned from the screen and faced him, 'Last night, Calder had a violent nightmare. He was fighting his monster.'

'So?'

'After the nightmare or maybe in continuation of it, he tried to steal an Eagle. I had to stun him.'

'John, I don't see . . .'

'He's just come round. He said he was on his way to face it.'

'The monster?'

'Those could be the same ships he saw beyond Ultra. If they are, we could be facing the danger he faced.'

Koenig turned to Sandra Benes, 'Increase magnification. Search around.'

Bergman was silent. The rest, reacting to Koenig's seriousness watched the scanner zoom and search among the silent ships.

Bergman found an objection, 'But we're light years away from Ultra.'

'Nothing's static. They didn't come from Ultra. They moved there and could move again. This Moon's a living proof. We moved. They could move.'

'But the coincidence?'

'If we never knew it before, we know now that nothing's impossible. Something triggered Calder. Something we have to take very seriously. Kano?'

'Commander?'

'Have Computer search the record of the Ultra Probe 1996. The flight recorder picked up contacts similar to those. I want to know if they're the same. Sandra?'

This time there was no reply. Totally committed to a delicate tuning ploy, she was on the edge of a discovery. Excitedly she called, 'Commander, it's here. I've found it!'

In two strides, Koenig was behind her chair watching the tiny image clarify on her ranging screen. Then she was pressing buttons to make the transfer and the big screen had a blow-up. Awed by her own act, she said, 'The Ultra Probeship!'

There was no area of doubt. It was there, silent and lifeless, with the emblem of the Space Commission at the waist. A piece of Earth in a foreign field.

Bergman said, 'It's incredible.'

'So was Calder's story of the monster –' Koenig called across to Carter, 'Alan, I want a docking Eagle on Pad One. And an escort of three. Ready for action.'

'Check, Commander.'

On the way out, Carter passed two new arrivals coming in. Jim Calder, zipped into uniform and holding himself tall, was walking calmly beside Helena. He crossed the floor and stood facing the big screen, impassive, unemotional, just looking at the Probeship with its missing command module. Without a change of expression, he stated a fact.

'So I get a second chance.' To Paul Morrow, he said, 'Any sign of life?'

'Not a thing. We've scanned the whole area. Negative.'

'There never was.'

Koenig said, 'I'm taking an Eagle up, with an armed escort of three. We'll scan it at closer and closer range. If Victor's absolutely convinced there's no danger in the area or on board, we'll dock on the Probeship. Does that make sense to you?'

All eyes were on Calder. Would he baulk at a plan which could confound his story? He understood well enough what was in every head; but he was icily calm, 'Sounds fine.'

'Would you be willing to come with me?'

There was something of his old charm in the smile, 'More than willing, John, I'd insist.'

Walking with Calder to the embarkation point, Victor Bergman was almost apologetic, 'You have to forgive me, Jim. It was too much for my logical mind to accept. But John, you know, never doubted. He was with you all the way through.'

Two paces behind, Helena Russell touched Koenig's arm to slow him. She was suddenly anxious, 'I don't trust him, John. He's unnaturally calm.'

'He has the chance to clear himself – after all this time.'

'I don't like it. Please be careful.'

In the Eagle, Alan Carter was already in the command module. Helena and Bergman settled themselves in front of the scanning and monitoring equipment. Koenig touched Helena's arm, 'I'll be up front with Alan, but the first indication of anything out of the way I want to know about it.'

'Of course.'

Calder had roamed off to the hatch which connected with the command cabin and said, 'Excuse me, folks. I owe Alan an apology.'

He went through and was out of sight. Koenig was behind Helena's chair, hands on her shoulders, watching her neat, economical movements as she brought the console to life and prepared to search for life signs on the hulks. He said, 'Concentrate on particular ships as we go in. See what computer has to say about them.'

Alan Carter was running through pre-lift off procedures when Calder joined him. He was not entirely easy with the relationship, though he had to concede that Calder had never stepped out of line as a subordinate. Not until the last phase.

Calder said, 'Alan I have to apologise about the other night. I'm sorry I clobbered you.'

Not one to bear a grudge, Carter waved it away, 'Not to worry. I'll believe it wasn't meant personally . . .' He turned in his seat to reinforce the message with a friendly grin and Calder did it again, chopping with the edge of his hand into Carter's neck.

Carter went out like a light and with fantastic strength Calder heaved him out of his bucket seat and dragged him to the communicating hatch. There was not far to go. It was all quick and neat with Koenig only looking up as the body thumped on the parquet behind him. As he whipped around, the command module hatch was sliding to close and sealed with a definitive click as he hurled himself across the gap.

In the pilot slot, Calder was working with speed and precision. He completed the check sequence and gunned the Eagle's motors. Then he hit the button for module separation. He was away, lifting from the pad with an Eagle frame, leaving the passenger module grounded and still attached to the boarding tube.

Koenig was snapping orders into his comlock. 'Eagles Three and Four, immediate lift off. Tail Calder in Eagle One. Eagle Two jettison module, move to Pad One and pick me up.'

Helena's monitor buzzed and she had Calder calm and determined on the screen. Without waiting for the question, he said, 'Sorry to do this, John. But it's my enemy. I deserve first crack.'

He was not prepared to argue. The screen blanked. Then he was away on a straight course for the distant collection of spacers with Eagles Three and Four hard on his heels.

Chafing at the delay, Koenig watched Eagle Two manoeuvre for position and drop slowly to the pad. Using his comlock, he spoke to Main Mission, 'Paul?'

'Commander?'

'You saw the action? Calder's trying to go it alone. Beam every scanner on him. If you have any information I want it right away.'

'Check, Commander.'

Koenig snapped his comlock shut and returned it to his belt. Helena was looking up at him from the deck where she was kneeling beside Carter. Her eyes mirrored an unspoken thought which he interpreted, 'You think he could be going ahead to destroy the evidence!'

Before she could reply, Carter was back in the world and had lifted his head. His hands went to his neck to rub the spot. A man with a justified grievance, he said, 'Will somebody tell me what that guy has against me?'

Green tell-tales glowed in the deckhead. The pilot of Eagle Two announced himself on Helena's console, 'Docking complete, Commander.'

Koenig was opening the hatch before the harmonics had stopped vibrating. He slammed into the co-pilot seat. 'Take it away. Give it everything you've got.'

Eagle Two jacked herself off the pad in a savage surge of power, came round on a course and sped away at full thrust in the wake of Calder and his escort.

The man himself sat at the controls of Eagle One as though on a routine patrol flight. He was utterly composed, made small finicky adjustments to the trim, betrayed no flicker of fear or anxiety. As he approached the great junk yard, he slowed, sheered away from a mammoth, dead hulk of a supership and had direct sight of the Ultra Probeship lying beyond.

There was little for Paul Morrow to report. 'He's close to the Probeship now, Commander. He's running about six minutes ahead of you.'

Koenig left the command module of Eagle Two to consult the onboard team. As he came through, Carter said, 'He *could* dock his command module on the Probeship.'

Bergman confirmed it, 'Part of the standardisation we aimed at, John. The control systems are compatible.'

Koenig turned to Helena. She said, 'We've got a detailed scan on. From Alpha, from here and from right up close through Eagles Three and Four. So far there's not a flicker. No life indications, no energy field, no radiation. Nothing.'

It seemed conclusive, certainly Koenig had no answer for it. Nor had Victor Bergman. He shook his head in response to Koenig's unspoken query.

There was something that did not gell. On the screen Calder's Eagle shadowed by Eagles Three and Four was closing on the hulk of the Probeship.

Koenig snapped on his comlock and called Main Mission, 'Paul?'

'Still nothing indicated, Commander.'

Balling a fist, Koenig thumped Helena's desk. 'Godammit, there has to be *something*. We're using more powerful gear than Calder had when he approached this lot before. But he's one hundred per cent right about those spaceships. Detail for detail spot on.'

There was one vital flaw in the implied argument and Helena put her finger on it. She said quietly, 'That doesn't *necessarily* mean he's right about the monster.'

It triggered a little of his old impatience with her for not seeing it exactly his way. He said sharply, 'You must concede that it makes him a whole lot more credible. Do *you* agree, Victor?'

There was something to be said on both sides. Victor Bergman shrugged without committing himself. They watched the unfolding scene on the scanner. Bergman relented, sensing that Koenig wanted him to say something. 'Sorry, John. Beyond the obvious explanation, I can't add anything.'

'What do you call obvious then?'

'Well, looking at those ships you have to say that they look like flies trapped in a web. But what web? As you see we can't isolate any force field or radiation belt.'

'Which brings us right back to Calder's monster. Ships get in there to investigate the mystery and they don't get out. Or those that get out don't report the hazard to Space Commission, Earth. How could they?'

Eagle Three came up on the net. 'Eagle Three to Eagle Two. Calder is separating the module now, Commander.'

Helena zoomed for a close look. They saw Eagle One's module easing out of the superstructure. Calder was putting on a faultless demonstration of technique.

Koenig called, 'Stay close, Three and Four. Keep the scan going.'

'Check, Commander, we're right with him.'

Calder's module edged delicately into line with the truncated shell of the Probeship. He was working with complete concentration like an extension of his machine. Centred to a millimetre, he backed home for a first time perfect docking.

Koenig briefed Carter, 'Go through and take the con, Alan. We'll dock on the Probeship's main hatch. Make it as smooth as Calder's we don't want to shake up the can.'

It got him a wry look from the two-time victim. Carter nipped smartly through the hatch.

Helena called, 'Life signs from the Probeship now, John ... Calder's.'

His disappointment was clear on his face, but she went on underlining the implications, 'It means that, if there was any other life form there, we'd be receiving indications.'

He knew it, but he was still fighting it, 'That's always supposing our instruments could read it.'

Time would reveal all. He could wait. Carter's voice sounded on the intercom, 'Docking in four minutes.'

Jim Calder thumped his harness release and heaved himself out of the pilot seat. The years between had dropped away. He was back where he had wanted to be. The long agony of the survival flight and the frustrations of long enquiries were so many dead leaves. He might never have left. Behind the hatch was Olga Vishonskya, who had been warm and beautiful and had been thrown contemptuously at his feet a lifeless husk. He was ice cold with the anger that had never died out of his mind.

Opening the crash locker, he spilled out the equipment. It was the axe he wanted and he found it clipped to the bulkhead at the back of the compartment. When he had it in his hand, he tested the weight and balance with a couple of practice swings. It would do. It would serve. This time . . . this time he would carve himself a path to wherever the monster kept its living nucleus.

He moved to the hatch, shoved down the opening stud and stood waiting, balanced on the balls of his feet with the axe ready to swing.

The hatch slid open. He was looking into the darkness of a cave with the light from the command module throwing his shadow forward. He padded through, making no noise with his foam soled boots. Olga's body was there, across his path, her face turned towards the hatch. There was enough light to see her face through the transparent mask of her visor. It was set like a wax model in her final scream of agony and fear.

It was no more than he had lived with in the long interlude. He stepped cautiously over the body and went on to seek his destiny. Even when he saw it, he felt no surprise. He had known for a sure truth that it would be there, coiled in an aconite's slumber.

The creature grew from a mound of shadow in the centre of the Ward Room floor. Tentacles wrapped round its octopoid mass, it was conserving its life force in a long hibernation. As Calder edged warily towards it, there was a slight ripple over its dark, shapeless bulk. Data acquisition networks were alerting the central office.

Firefly points of light began to glow as though its eye function was diffused over the area of its head. The massive body was jacking itself out of torpor into consciousness.

Calder's eyes, narrow and watchful, ranged over the formless lump. The ends of the tentacles were beginning to stir. He moved round. He saw the bodies of Juliet Mackie and Darwin King lying where they had fallen. He was close in, partly screened by one of the module's fixed seats.

A tentacle writhed out slowly across the deck and was a metre off when he stepped out deliberately and hacked down with a two handed blow. Then he was back behind his cover.

It was the end of lethargy. The creature blazed into angry action. The wounded tentacle thrashed wildly and then wrapped itself round the back of the chair. With a surge of power it heaved away and tore the fitting from its holding bolts. The main body was gaping into a coldly burning hole, a screeching wind was trying to suck the intruder deep into the maw.

Calder's face showed only exhilaration. All doubts and complications were long gone. He was the archetypal hunter facing the ultimate quarry. He seemed to want to infuriate it further. Feeling around the deck, he picked up items of loose gear and hurled them into the glowing ring of the notional mouth.

They were hurled out like projectiles. His eyes were adjusting to the half light and he could pick out the feeler he had wounded at the first encounter. It was deformed and slow moving. He shifted to that side, jabbing with his axe and the monster turned to bring itself to a stance where other tentacles could plug the gap in its defences. Calder moved with it and there was a slow circle.

Calder was weighing up the angles, he wanted to get close. Back to a bulkhead for extra purchase, he shoved off in a jump that took him along the wounded feeler.

It twisted to encircle him, but had lost tension and flexibility. Other tentacles were coming from awkward angles and lacked their usual force. He beat them away with wheeling axe blows and crowded in until he could grip the pocked and knobbly skin of the monster's tossing head.

Koenig's Eagle slid home on the Probeship's main hatch. Carter left his pilot seat and came through. All hands were waiting for the moment of truth.

Koenig handed out stun guns from the rack. He said, 'Great work, Alan.'

He tried the instrumentation one more time. 'Life signs, Helena?'

'Still only Calder's and they've gone crazy.'

'No other problems?'

'Nothing. The Probeship module is pressurised and atmosphere controlled.'

They lined up at the hatch. Koenig, Carter, two security files, Helena and Bergman. As Koenig shoved the stud for the air lock, each looked to their laser settings and armed for destructor beams.

As they went through, light from the Eagle doubled the lumen count in the Probeship's module. The action was plain to see and was as bizarre as it could well get.

Calder was high on the monster's back. Holding on with one hand, he was beating down with his axe to breach the carapace and was sending the writhing turbulent mass into a paroxysm of frenzy.

Outlined by the light at their backs, the newcomers stopped in amazement to take in a scene that was straight from the pages of fable.

The monster went suddenly still to check them out. The flaming mouth turned to them with a demented shriek. Calder seized his chance. His platform was suddenly steady. Standing feet astride, he swung his axe for a tremendous blow into the obscene head. The blade bit deep. Black slime welled from the cut as he wrenched the axe free. There was a violent shudder that cost him his balance and he pitched forward past the gaping mouth to fall to the deck.

Tentacles flashed in to enwrap him. His axe dropped from his hands. Struggling to the last, he was lifted and thrust into the crematorium.

Koenig was moving in, firing and backed by fire from every laser. There was no impact. They might have been feeding it candy bars. Koenig dropped his laser and ran on. He had seen the axe. His hands were closing on it as Calder's lifeless husk was tossed out to the deck.

The tentacles were moving beside and beyond him writhing towards the source of the laser beams. He yelled, 'Keep firing!'

Helena's agonised shout, 'John. Come back!' was lost in the frenetic screeching that was notching to a crescendo.

But he was standing four square in front of the hole feeling the tug of suction and seeing the ooze of black slime dimming some of the firefly lights. The head lowered. He raised the axe and went for the breach Calder had made.

The shining blade buried itself to the haft. There was a gush of viscous, black ooze. The glow from the open mouth dimmed and the hole closed. There was a shuddering groan and the monster sank to a slack mound in a spreading pool of uliginous pitch.

Koenig moved slowly to the hatch, gestured for the others to go through and then stood holding the coaming. All that was left of Jim Calder had come to rest an armslength from Olga Vishenskya. It was done. Calder had sought his destiny and found it.

He went through to the Eagle and shoved the stud to seal the hatch. Helena Russell came forward to meet him. He said, 'Doubting Helena.' But there was no malice in it, only infinite compassion for the human situation they were all in.

Her head went to his chest and he held her tightly. Over her blonde head, he said soberly, 'That wraps it up. Take us home, Alan. Have Eagle Three co-pilot pick up Eagle One and the module. Then destroy the Probeship.'

They saw it on the scanner, with Moonbase Alpha coming close. The armed Eagles homed in for a strike and the Ultra Probeship made its last spectacular gesture, opening in a brilliant asterisk of white light as the searing laser beams probed into the target.

Helena Russell made a final paragraph on her report-saga. Koenig watched her, sitting on a low chair in her personal niche in Moonbase Alpha's sprawling complex. The scanners in Main Mission probed endlessly in their search, but here at least was a temporary home – their island in the eye of the wind.

She wrote, *'The monster was beyond anything we would have believed. According to our criteria it was never alive, so how could we ever be sure it was dead? We did what we could to prevent future spacefarers being trapped. The great graveyard of empty ships dwindled on the scanners as our Moon's divergent course separated us forever from the Dragon's Domain.'*

She slipped the sheet from the machine and handed it to Koenig, flushed a little from the throes of literary composition and unsure of its reception.

She said defensively, 'You know, John, if we ever do find a

new place to live and if we succeed in founding a new civilisation, we're going to need a brand new mythology.'

'So we have Jim Calder And The Monster for starters? Does it have quite the right ring to it?'

'Saint George and the Dragon sounds pretty flat until you know the story.'

Koenig looked at her affectionately. He knocked the sheets of the report into a tidy pile and said, 'Our first literary genius. Who knows what twists will get incorporated into this in the fullness of time. The story is part of our history. I think Jim would settle for that. He'd be very happy to know that he'd breathed new life into an old myth.'

Helena moved over to sit on the arm of his chair. She said, 'I think, now, I understand how I got the details. More mythology if you like. I've been talking to Victor. He thinks we tracked through an eddy in space and caught up with vibes from that past time. Calder was specially sensitive and picked them up as he lay unconscious and they were transmitted to me as I sat beside him.'

'Impressions can get transmitted when people sit next to people.'

'There have been misunderstandings enough. I wouldn't like you to get any wrong impressions.'

Her fair head nestled silkily against his left ear.

Koenig thought that the statistical likelihood of the right man and the right woman meeting on an errant Moon in deep space was of the same order as finding his planet amongst the myriad stars. He reckoned soberly it was a good omen and dropped her literary masterpiece, with all due respect, to her oatmeal carpet.

CHAPTER NINE

Stylised combat was a great therapy for suppressed energy and Koenig joined with the rest in an enthusiastic resurrection of the ancient art of quarterstaffs, updated and renamed Kendo with a courtly etiquette and a book of rules.

He reckoned it was a useful safety valve to let one and all take a crack at the command figure and every shrewd thump at his padding was so much psychological gain. Few, in fact, got through his guard or could match his quick reaction times. One who could was Luke Ferro, a powerfully built man, who could move like a cat and was always ready with a challenge as though for him, particularly, knocking hell out of the Commander was an end in itself.

More than most, Ferro was constrained by the physical limits of Moonbase Alpha. He had not joined as an astronaut. When the Moon took off, he was there on a photographic survey.

Anna Davis was another such, though, by temperament, she had settled more easily into the isolated community. As a research student in the origins of language, isolation was her meat and she was working on a comprehensive survey of Earth languages, so that when the Alphans finally set up their tent poles, no nuance of their linguistic past would be lost. She irritated and fascinated Luke Ferro. She rated him an uncouth barbarian and when he was not trying to thump Koenig with his Kendo staff, as a symbol of the top brass he was using him as a surrogate for the refined and elegant linguist, in the hope of cracking her icy veneer and provoking an earthy response.

Feet flapping on the mat in the recreation area, eyes narrowed behind the slit in his protective face mask, Ferro bored in for a strike. It was a ferocious work out and both men were breathing hard. The bleep from the communications post took a second to break into their concentration. Koenig felt that he had been saved by the bell.

Paul Morrow on the screen was looking tense. 'Commander, Main Mission. Urgent.'

Koenig lifted his face mask, 'Check. I'll be right there.'

He picked up a robe and draped it over his shoulders,

pitching his staff for Ferro to catch. 'Your point, Luke, without a doubt.'

'Another time, Commander.'

'My pleasure.'

In Main Mission, every desk had its executive. Sensitised by his work out, Koenig felt the tension like a physical presence. Victor Bergman was frowning at a data sheet. The rest were staring at the big screen.

Koenig moved in behind Morrow at the command desk. Sandra had isolated a distant system. There was a small planet with a pale glow and away beyond it, the tiny dot of its hot, red sun. He thought, 'Here we go again. This could be the one. One day, it will start like this and we shall have found what we are looking for.'

Aloud he said, 'Easy all. What's the problem?'

Morrow picked up a clipboard and handed it over. Koenig glanced at it and he could understand their reactions. Startled himself, he looked at Morrow for confirmation, then he was checking the sheet again in simple disbelief. It was all there and not good.

'Sandra, what's our position?'

'Eight point five degrees relative, Commander. There's no mistake. Our course is altering.'

It earned her a sceptical look, 'But we're nowhere near the gravitational pull of that planet.'

Victor Bergman came to her defence, 'John, no gravitational or magnetic factors are involved.'

'So you've been working on it. What *is* causing it?'

'I have to tell you, John, that we simply don't know.'

'Let's find out. Sandra, activate long range sensors.'

Sandra Benes tried. For thirty seconds, there was silence as her delicate fingers roved over the instrument spread. Koenig knew if anybody could do it, she was that same one. There was no joy. She said suddenly, 'Scanner malfunction.' Something else registered, she went on urgently, 'And there's a power loss.'

Koenig snapped out, 'Kano . . . ?'

Kano had needed no prompting, he was already asking the box. A puzzled man, he turned to Koenig, 'Something is wrong with the generators, Commander.'

'Trace it.'

All hands watched him work a trouble-shooting sequence.

The generators were Alpha's beating heart. Everything stemmed from the power they gave, heat, light, food, atmosphere. Name anything that gave Moonbase Alpha a toehold on survival and it could be traced back to the power house.

Kano was apologetic, 'I can't isolate anything, but the power loss is confirmed. Looking straight at Koenig, he went on, 'There's a five per cent power loss right across the board, Commander.'

If Kano said it, then it had to be right. Koenig left the horseshoe of executive desks and walked over to a direct vision port. To the naked eye, the starmap was unchanged, but the Moon was rushing them forward into some unknown hazard. The only sure thing was that they had no way of avoiding it. Whatever they were getting into, would have to be endured.

Kano called, 'Power loss rate now hitting seven percent.'

Koenig joined Victor Bergman. A glance at his face showed how seriously he was taking it. Paul Morrow asked, 'Commander, do we alert all sections?'

'Not yet, Paul. Get Carter and Helena Russell in here and ... Kano keep checking that power loss.'

Morrow hit the intercom button and Main Mission shivered through every centimetre of its fabric. He checked along the desk. Voice cracking with disbelief, he jerked out, 'The Moon ... we're slowing up!'

'That's not possible!' Bergman had joined him at the command console.

In a flurry of activity, every operator made an independent check. Main Mission was rocking to its foundations. Holding on to his chair Morrow said, 'There's no mistake, Commander. We're definitely slowing.'

Koenig had his arm crooked round a stanchion and was glaring at the big screen for any sign of activity from the planet and its sun. There was nothing. He called, 'Sandra! Are we picking up anything from that planet ... anything at all?'

Her voice was edged with rising panic, 'Nothing, Commander. Negative. Long range probes are affected by the power loss.'

They were almost cut back to simple, physical estimates. Their wandering cinder heap had developed a rocking motion. Kinaesthetically, they felt it was grinding to a halt.

129

Kano had more bad news, 'We're still losing power. Loss rate now eight percent.'

Motion was exaggerated. They were swaying like puppets in a box. There was a violent shudder and silence as everyone looked around for confirmation of what he knew in his bones had happened. The swaying had died away. Paul Morrow looked up from his console and made it official in a flat statement. 'Commander ... the Moon has stopped dead.'

From the direct vision ports of Koenig's command office, the moonscape and the starmap were unchanged. But the knowledge that they were held motionless was pervasive and disquieting. With the Moon in headlong motion, there was a sense of progress. Every minute covered distance and sometime, somehow there was the hope of a landfall. Now they were thrown back on the survival prospects of Moonbase Alpha and those were being steadily eroded.

Koenig looked from Helena Russell to Victor Bergman.

Bergman said slowly, 'Gravity or magnetic forces ... *could* affect the course and velocity of an object the size of the Moon.'

Helena finished it for him '. . . But they couldn't stop us cold in space like this.'

Victor Bergman was positive, '*Nothing* we know of could do that.'

'Then there has to be something we don't know of.' Koenig crossed to his desk and sat on the edge of it. 'There has to be a third force and I think it has something to do with that planet out there.'

The communications post blipped for attention and Kano appeared on the screen, 'Commander, we've run every possible test on the reactors and generators.'

'And?'

'We can't trace any faults, but ...'

'But what, Kano?'

'We're still losing power, Commander. Loss rate now eleven per cent.'

Koenig thumped his desk top.

'How can that be, dammit, if there's nothing wrong with our power units?'

'Computer can only define it as fault due to external forces.'

'External forces! God damn the idiot's tin guts. Can't it be more specific?'

Kano was affronted for his friend. Heatedly he said, 'Computer is not a crystal ball, Commander. It can only predict on the basis of specific data and there's a marked absence of that!'

It was unusual to have Kano losing his cool and it brought Koenig down to earth. He said more calmly, 'All right, Kano. Thank you.'

He called Paul Morrow. 'What's the situation, Paul?'

Main Mission's Controller could give no comfort, 'Alpha is feeling the effects of power loss, Commander. A kind of creeping paralysis. So far only the power-intensive, long range systems are right out – but it's getting worse by the minute.'

Koenig shoved himself off the desk. Activating his comlock, he opened the hatch to Main Mission and strode in followed by Bergman and Helena Russell. There was a subdued atmosphere. Every executive was busy at his desk, but clearly reckoning that it was unnecessary now.

Stopping at Sandra's console, Koenig said shortly, 'How long do we have?'

Trim and efficient, she put it on the line, 'At the present rate of power loss, we have thirty-eight hours, Commander. Economies across the board would give us ten hours more.'

It was an easy sum. Koenig said it for his own satisfaction, 'Forty-eight hours . . . Alan, how much flying time to the planet?'

That was more complex and Alan Carter used the Eagle Command computer.

'Thirty hours for a round trip.'

'Thirty hours. All right. We'll take a team down. Victor, I'll need you for scientific assessment. Helena – medical and environment. Two security files to ride shotgun – Kano, have computer select two others with a wide spectrum of outside knowledge to make up the number.'

'Check, Commander.'

Koenig turned to his two leading specialists, 'With our long range systems on the blink, we won't have access to main computer, so make sure we have everything we'll need on the surface.'

They were away and he briefed his chief pilot, 'Alan, arm and provision Eagle One for an eight man team . . . we're leaving now.'

He had still not finished.

'Paul. Phased power shutdown. All the economies you can make stick. Right away.'

Main Mission slipped easily into top gear like a well oiled machine. Sandra Benes checked for another estimate of power loss. There was a reading of thirteen per cent.

Morrow began an all stations call and Alphans moving about the halls and covered ways of the sprawling base, stopped in their tracks to get the message. His face was on every communications post screen, serious and intent, *'This is Controller Paul Morrow. We have an emergency power situation and for the present economies are vital.'*

Koenig and his party heard it as they headed for the travel tube exit which would take them out to Eagle One's pad. Beside Helena and Bergman, he had Irwin and N'Dole as security cover and computer had come up with a curious choice for the two extras. Luke Ferro was there, with his easy looselimbed walk and a camera hung round his neck. The other was Anna Davis, neat and precise and walking beside him without giving him a look, as though her mind was pondering on the vagaries of the *umlaut*.

Morrow's voice continued as they waited for Carter to go through exit drills.

'These economies will be phased to deal with the continuing situation. Strict observance is a necessity. Phase One. The following activities are cancelled until further notice . . .'

It was a poor note on which to leave Alpha. There was silence as the travel tube accelerated away.

Main Mission watched them board the waiting Eagle and Morrow was on the air again to control the lift off.

'Eagle One, you are clear.'

Carter, in the pilot seat, answered on the net and fed in some power. Eagle One rose in a flurry of moon dust, circled to pick up a course and was away in its race against the clock.

John Koenig, in the co-pilot slot, had time on his hands for a further dialogue with Main Mission's Controller and kept it a one-to-one personal link.

'What's the situation, Paul?'

'The power loss rate seems to be consistent with the projection. So the figures we gave you still hold – forty-eight hours.'

'Thanks, Paul. We'll hurry it along. We'll be back as soon as we can.'

All told, it was all anybody could undertake to do. Koenig reckoned that he had left Morrow with the harder task. Behind him, Bergman was thoughtful, making notes on a pad, still trying to explain the unexplainable to himself. At his side, Helena Russell was checking a box of sample slides.

Irwin and N'Dole farther along the car were overhauling hand guns and rocket rifles, not much to tackle a planet with, but they would at least be ready for an attack. In the rumble, Luke Ferro was the only drone. He had his feet up on the squab ahead and he was looking at his diminished image in the lens of his camera.

This pursuit was not impressing his companion. Anna Davis, serious and methodical, was freshening up on the print-out, data sheets of the mystery planet. Catching sight of his big feet over the top of her file, she gave a delicate shudder and resumed her concentrated scan.

It was not lost on Luke. He grinned widely, clamped the viewfinder on his camera and swung round to get her in close-up.

In spite of a massive effort to ignore him, it was all there in peripheral vision and a slow blush built up along her cheek bones.

'Do you have to do that?'

'I'm studying the angles in case the opportunity should arise to use you in a bubble bath commercial.'

It got him a slow burn which did nothing to diminish his grin. Koenig's voice on the intercom saved her reply.

Koenig said, 'We have a long ride. When we get there, we'll need all our wits. Get some sleep while you can.'

He followed it up by coming through the command module hatch and taking a place on the squab next to Helena. They sat in silence and he took her neat, capable, surgeon's hand. The hurrying Eagle arrowed across the starmap.

In Main Mission, Sandra Benes forced herself to make the next timed check on the power systems. The monitor still carried the legend from her last survey. POWER LOSS RATE 13%. She completed the sequence and got a silvery chime from the switchgear. The screen whited out and then glowed with the latest SitRep POWER LOSS RATE 16%.

Kano joined her in a silent query to Paul Morrow. It was no

more than confirmation of the rate he had extrapolated, but intellectual satisfaction was no pleasure. He said quietly, 'There's no choice, Sandra. Activate phase three power cuts.'

Except for Koenig, who was looking haggard from a long stint in the pilot seat, there was more relaxation in Eagle One. The passenger module was bathed in a restful, low-key light. Anna Davis, as demure sleeping as waking had shifted sideways and her neat head, with no hair out of place had chocked itself comfortably on Luke's left shoulder. First to open his eyes, he grinned appreciatively. Taken close, it was a pleasant visitor to have. He reckoned her reaction would make his day. Without disturbing her, he settled himself for another doze.

He missed by a fraction the sign that flashed on over the command module hatch – EAGLE ONE IN ORBIT.

Koenig was watching his scanner. It was shortly before sunset on the slice of planet surface that was currently peeling away below the hurrying Eagle. A round red disc was standing like a penny on the horizon. The landscape was desolate, with jutting clumps of bare rock and isolated thickets of leafless, petrified trees. He told himself that he could be looking at a bad patch, the local Kalahari, but it was a poor omen. It was not the promised land for the Alphans. He shoved down a stud. A musical chime alerted his team.

Luke Ferro watched his sleeping partner jerk back into the world of sense and relished her maidenly confusion. He asked, 'Sleep well, then?'

There was a dignified withdrawal along the squab and an embarrassed silence.

In the command module, Alan Carter moved out of sleep into instant activity, checking his instrument spread in mid yawn.

Koenig said, 'Take over, Alan.'

'Anything?'

'No. Not yet.'

Koenig thumped his harness release stud and heaved himself out of his seat. He went through into the passenger module and Helena looked her question.

He said, 'We've circled the planet twice and so far we've seen no signs of habitation, no unusual structures, nothing that suggests intelligent life – but we're still looking.'

It was strange – if the planet was the source of the Moon's erratic behaviour – and it was disappointing. Koenig sat down, rubbing his face with both hands as though to wear away a sour skin of tiredness. All hands moved to stations. Helena paused long enough to stroke Koenig's bent head and then took her place beside Victor Bergman to process the data he was pulling in from the sensors.

Luke Ferro was taking a series of stills as Carter took Eagle One in a low run over a stark, lifeless plain with the same outcrops of grey rock and trees that looked as though no bird had ever nested in their lifeless limbs. Sitting beside him, Anna Davis collected the frames and identified them for assembly.

Carter watched the scene unroll from his direct vision ports and called Koenig, 'We're wasting our time, Commander. It's just desolation out there.'

Koenig had the same view from the passenger module. He said, 'All right, Alan. Steady as you go.'

He stretched wearily and joined Bergman, 'What have you got, Victor?'

'This *was* a living world . . . once . . . but something happened, some terrible catastrophe overtook it which obliterated all life.'

Helena added, 'From the radioactive trace elements in the atmosphere I'd guess at some kind of holocaust in the distant past.'

'So the planet is uninhabitable?'

'Not quite. The atmosphere has stabilised now. Radiation is down to tolerable levels.'

'Stabilised? How do you arrive at that? There's no cycle of plant life to leave free oxygen.'

'True, but there are no agencies at work using it up. As I see it, the atmosphere remains much as it was at the point when life stopped.'

It was an argument that could go on and Koenig reckoned that time was not on their side. 'Then we'd better get down there to find some real answers, before life stops on Alpha.' He called the driver. 'Take her down, Alan.'

There was a thinning of darkness as Alan Carter wheeled Eagle One in a tight turn, looking for a planetfall. When he touched down in a flurry of dry dust it was darker at ground level but there was a sense of impending dawn.

When they opened the hatch and stepped out to the surface

there was an overwhelming sense of desolation.

One place was as good as another. Koenig said shortly, 'Off-load what gear you need. We'll set up by that rock face. As fast as you like.'

They moved it along with a will. They were in a limbo that oppressed the mind. Action was a welcome relief. When the stores were out, they had the rough beginnings of a base camp. Koenig called them together, 'Each pair will investigate an area. If for any reason you move off line, let security know about it. Stay with your partner and maintain the comlock link at all times. One final thing . . . I don't have to labour this one . . . the fate of Alpha, all of us for that matter, depends on what answers we come up with. That's about it.'

Bergman and Helena shouldered their packs and moved off. Anna Davis, watched by Luke, took a precise compass reading and they went off, together. Irwin and N'Dole brought out the last necessary gear and Irwin reported to Koenig. 'That's everything you wanted, Commander.'

'Fine. You know the drill. We'll call in as arranged. Keep on alert.'

'We'll do that, Commander.'

'Ready, Alan? We take designated area seven.'

As they moved off, they could see their Moon, eerily similar to its aspect when viewed from Earth. But there the likeness ended. From a rising hillock, they could see the landscape in bright starlight, dotted with jagged rock formations and clumps of dead trees. A thin band of pale viridian marked the beginning of day.

There was no more to see from the next rise or the next. What he was looking for, Koenig could not have said precisely. The only sure thing was that it didn't seem likely to be anywhere around.

At a third hill, Koenig stopped. He said, 'It's hard to believe that this place was once alive with trees stirring, grazing animals, maybe intelligent life organising itself.'

'We came a few thousand years too late.'

'Well, there's no profit on this line. Let's get back and see what the instruments have to say.'

Anna and Luke Ferro had hit the edge of a large petrified copse. For the record, Ferro made a photoscan of individual trees and Anna Davis, kneeling on the deck, searched methodically for remnants of dry, preserved leaf forms. A small, sad dawn wind seemed to have localised itself in the ancient grove.

Luke, still batting conversationally in spite of negative response, said, 'I've come to realise this is no tropical paradise with humming birds and that; but this place really gets to me.'

Anna went on working, studying a leaf and comparing it with a reference kit. He went on, 'Still, after living on Alpha, I guess any open space can seem strange.'

She was still working on her samples, but her manner, even for a controlled and orderly subject, looked tense and excited.

'What do you have, then? A bread fruit tree?'

'Luke, scan the trees just here.'

It was progress. She wanted him. He moved over, all agog.

Helena Russell and Victor Bergman were at the mouth of a cave. Light was strengthening all the time, but it brought no improvement to the landscape.

Bergman looked around in disgust, 'The scenery doesn't change much, does it?'

She was busy with her geiger counter. Radiation was low. The planet was ready to start again on the long cycle of growth and decay. She said, 'Crops might grow but the soil's dead. Totally devoid of bacteria. It would take a long time to get things growing.'

'That's one thing we don't have ... time.'

She stood in the cave entrance. There was more light by the minute as though a curtain was being run back. Bergman joined her and they went in. Ten metres from the entrance there was a dog leg twist and they moved cautiously into it not relishing the feel of the place. Then their eyes were adjusting to the lumen count and any reservations they had were justified in full measure.

It was a large, vault-like burrow. The walls were covered from floor to roof with close set inscriptions. It was like being set down in a hole in a book. But the centre tableau held their eye and froze them with a shock of horror. They had come across the people of the country and they were not going to answer any questions. There were eight skeletal forms sitting erect at an endless board meeting. The debate was long finished. The ashen light gave the bare bones and grinning skulls a sickening glow.

Having had one as a companion for many years when a medical student, Helena Russell had no difficulty in recognising the genre. She said, '*Human* skeletons!'

Koenig reckoned the cave as the nearest thing to a break in the blank face of the planet that they had and concentrated all hands in the area. Bergman worked on the painted texts. He said, 'How much do you know about ancient Earth languages, John?'

'*Earth* languages?'

'Unless I'm mistaken these inscriptions are in Sanskrit.'

It made no kind of sense. Helena Russell left a heap of bones and joined them looking startled.

Koenig said, 'Sanskrit?'

'Yes, the basic proto-European root language, Sanskrit — the mother of tongues.'

'Are you sure?'

'Not sure, but the similarity is there.'

Helena said, 'John . . . Anna Davis would know. This is her field.'

'What?' It was almost too much for coincidence. He said, slowly, 'Computer chose better than it knew.'

He flipped open his comlock, 'Anna, get here right away.'

There was a pause until footsteps sounded down the echoing ante room and she came in with a rush followed by Luke Ferro.

Both stopped. It was all new to them, but it seemed to hit them harder than anybody yet.

Anna Davis's voice was an awed whisper, 'What is this place?'

Koenig said quietly, 'Over here, Anna.' He pointed to the wall. 'Here's something we need your opinion on.'

For a beat, she studied the surface, hand to her mouth. Then she took a half step back into Luke Ferro. 'I don't believe it.'

'Sanskrit?'

'Sanskrit. Yes . . . but different, somehow . . . an earlier form perhaps . . . , but how can that be, here, a million light years from Earth . . . how?'

'We don't know. Not yet. Can you decipher it?'

'Without the use of the main computer it will take time . . . yes, I think so.'

'Okay, get to it.'

Luke Ferro was staring as though transfixed at the skeleton chairman. His expression was an odd mixture of fear and fascination. If the bony structure had been clothed in flesh and granted eyeballs, it would have appeared that he was being hypnotised.

Koenig said sharply, 'Luke! Luke, are you okay?'

The words took time to penetrate. Luke Ferro seemed to make a big physical effort to break away. He said, 'Yes . . . fine . . .' He looked over at the wall, back to the quiet skeletons and then back to Koenig who was watching him narrowly.

He said, 'I'll help Anna.'

Far away, in Main Mission, Paul Morrow had pulled out a backgammon board and was playing Kano in a vicious, positive game. Minutes were peeling off the clock like lead strips. The monitor now read POWER LOSS RATE 26%.

Morrow held up his throw to hit a switch for a new check. It read, POWER LOSS RATE 30%. With a grim look at Kano, he called the base on the PA net. *'Attention all sections Alpha. This is Controller Paul Morrow . . .'*

Tanya crossed his line of vision as she came in with an armful of heavy sweaters and he held the line open while he caught one. She said, 'Here, this will keep your dice hand supple.'

Morrow went on, *'Phase Four power reductions now operative. Until further notice, travel tube facilities between Alpha Sections 1 to 4 are suspended. Heating will be automatically reset to number four and Moonbase lighting systems will reduce to half power.'*

Alphans, listening at communications posts, took it in gloomy silence. Lights slowly dimmed. As Morrow shrugged into his sweater, the medicentre direct line buzzed and Mathias appeared on the monitor screen. 'Paul, I know you've got problems, but I must have more power. I've got patients here who'll freeze to death.'

Morrow's head reappeared through the neck hole. He said, 'Sandra, allocate four extra units to the medicentre.'

It pleased Mathias, with a 'Thanks' he switched himself off the link. Paul Morrow went on, *'Reduce heating in Main Mission by four units.'*

Sandra said, 'Check, Controller.' If she was due to freeze, she would stick to protocol. She watched Morrow take up the game. She had never seen him look so frustrated. Kano said, 'Don't worry . . . it can only get worse.'

On the planet surface, Luke Ferro and Anna Davis were

139

working smoothly together on the only lead that had come up. Luke had refined an aerial photograph technique to cover the walls with a picture grid. They had cleared the table of its dead and Anna was using his magnified print-outs as a continuous text and running the take through a computer scan which Victor Bergman had improvised.

Intent and absorbed, she seemed to be reconciled to the ominous brooding stillness in the heart of the rock.

Luke took a final section and joined her at the table.

'How's it going?'

'If only we had access to the reference library.'

He pointed to the pile of old bones, 'And if they could talk, we'd know how they died. Have we learned anything?'

'Let me get on and I might be able to tell you!'

There was no sting in the protest and her smile was for an ally or even a fellow conspirator.

'Sorry.'

'Don't mind me. I get really involved.'

'You're right, of course. The sooner you're finished, the quicker we can get out of this place.'

Koenig and Carter joined the rest of the party in the camp area where Helena was already repacking some of her equipment.

Bergman asked, 'Any luck, John?'

'Not a thing. Nothing we've seen could have caused what's happening on Alpha. Helena . . . those skeletons?'

'They were humanoid . . . pretty much like ourselves. The bones show they died of radiation, somewhere between twenty and twenty-five thousand years ago.'

It got him no further. Thoughtfully, he said, 'There's something about that cave that bugs me. Let's get back there.'

It was not doing anything for Luke Ferro either. When Koenig and the others rejoined, he was listening to Anna's tentative translation and darting nervous glances around the area.

She read out, 'To you . . . who seek us out . . . by the . . . I think it's *ages* . . . yes . . . in the *ages* to come. I . . . something – a proper name possibly . . . guardian . . . salute you. The desolation you find . . . distresses . . . no, not distresses – grieves we few who will soon die.'

Her clear, quiet voice was at odds with the macabre death pit. After another reference to the print-out, she went on, 'We are an unfortunate or *accursed* people. Our civilisation gone. Our world Arkane . . . Arkad . . . no, Arkadia – our world Arkadia, poisoned, dying. We who caused our own . . . death? . . . No I don't think it's death . . .'

Bergman said softly, 'Destruction?'

'Yes, that could be it – destruction, have paid the price of ignorance and greed. No need now to tell of that final event . . . happening . . .?'

Everybody wanted to help, Helena said, 'Disaster . . . holocaust?'

'That's it . . . the final holocaust when our world burned in the inferno of a thousand . . . no, ten thousand, exploding suns.'

She stopped and looked at Koenig, 'There's more of this. The imagery is very difficult.'

'You're doing more than well, go on.'

'Arkadia is finished . . . but she will live on . . . the bodies . . .? the hearts and minds of some few of our . . . most precious . . . aware?'

'Enlightened?' Koenig added his bit.

'Right! *Enlightened* people, who left before the end . . . taking the best . . . the something of a new beginning.'

Luke came to with an effort of will, 'Seeds.'

'Seeds of a new beginning. To seek and find or begin. I think it's begin. Yes. Seek out and begin again in the distant regions of space. Heed now the Testament of Arkadia.'

She paused and leaned back. Luke Ferro put a hand on her shoulder. Surprisingly she covered it with her own and then gently disengaged to get back to work. 'There's a passage here, I can't make sense of. I'll need the memory banks in main computer. Then it goes on . . . You who are sent, no *guided*. You who are *guided* here, make the land fertile . . . help us to live once more . . . help us to live again. Farewell.'

There was a digestive silence. Finally, Koenig said, 'Human skeletons. An Earth language. People from Earth in this place, twenty-five thousand years ago.'

Helena Russell said, 'We know that's impossible, John.'

Bergman agreed, 'Our ancestors were enterprising enough. They were just inventing the wheel. But space travel? No. Not on!'

There was a gasp from Luke Ferro and every eye tracked round to him. He was tense, quivering with a curious emotion.

He said, 'No! Earth people did not come here. The Arkadians . . . they found Earth.'

Out and about, echoing round the quiet cave, it had the ring of revelation.

Koenig said, 'What makes you say that?'

'Ask Anna . . . she knows.' He bent down to her for support, 'Tell him, Anna . . . the trees. Tell him about the trees.'

She hesitated and he went on, 'The trees out there. We found Oak, Pine, Willow, Beech – forty different varieties of trees. Every one of them native to Earth.'

Anna Davis was looking at him enrapt as though seeing him for the first time. She nodded in confirmation.

Luke Ferro was inspired as he explained, 'You heard the inscription. The Arkadians took the seed with them. They found a new Arkadia. The planet Earth. This is our homeland. Our people originated *here* on this planet.'

CHAPTER TEN

Sunset in Arkadia was no improvement. The great disc of the sun was blood red and added another dimension of impending doom to the stark landscape. In the camp area, Koenig sipped his coffee, no nearer any kind of solution to the problem of Alpha's crippling dilemma. Alan Carter, knowing his mood, said diffidently, 'We're running out of time, Commander. We've got to get back to Alpha.'

There was no reply. Helena Russell handed the pilot a beaker of coffee. He said, 'Thanks, Doctor,' and continued to look at Koenig. When he got an answer it was on a different tack.

'We could bring life to this planet. The question is how long would it take to rejuvenate the soil? What do you think, Helena?'

'At least two years to establish crops.'

'So it's a straight calculation. If we evacuated Alpha, brought our people down here . . . how long have we got on the rations we could bring?'

'Over three hundred people . . . six months at the outside.'

'Six months.'

Victor Bergman showed the other side of the coin, 'With no power, Alpha will freeze to death in less than one day.'

'So it's a suicide run either way. But at least, here, we'd be buying a little time.'

Alan Carter said, 'Not a lot.'

For Koenig, the issues were crystal clear. He had no choice. He had to go for the better chance. He threw the dregs of his coffee on the ground. 'That is so. But time enough to hope for a miracle.'

Packing the last of the gear in the cave, Luke Ferro and Anna Davis were rushing to get away. More than any of the Alphans the atmosphere of the place had seized on their minds.

Luke Ferro, lifting a pack to the table, suddenly staggered and put both hands to his head. Anna, indifference to him long gone, dropped what she was doing and ran to him.

'Luke?'

Then she too, felt it. The cave was bending and distorting

before her eyes and a weird clatter of gibberish sounded in her ears.

Whatever the sense of it, the intonation suggested a question and it was repeated over and over. A light with no source seemed to settle around Luke's head and Anna could see that he, at least, was beginning to make sense of the message. The light expanded and included herself. Suddenly everything was plain.

The two were looking at each other, their hands stretched out, met and held. Around them, the inside of the cave was in a flux of change. They were rapt, ecstatic, radiant with a knowledge of each other and of a joint purpose.

The voice ceased. Normality returned. Anna looked at her hands and some of her normal reserve made her attempt to withdraw, but Luke pulled her close. His arms went round her. Slowly, her hands moved to lace themselves round the back of his head.

A bleep from Luke's comlock broke into their private world. Koenig's face appeared on the miniature screen. 'We've decided to abandon Alpha. Get back here right away.'

It chimed with their thinking. Joy and elation on their faces, they moved slowly to the cave entrance.

Alan Carter lifted Eagle One in a storm of dust and swept her away on a course for Alpha. They watched Arkadia dwindle in the direct vision ports. It was not at all what Koenig had imagined as the ultimate landfall for his people. Maybe some would make out. In some ways, it was spaceship *Daria* over again. But if he could have seen his base, he would have been more positive that he had made the only choice.

In Main Mission, staff were in Polar rig with frost crystals making patterns on the direct vision ports. Lights were low and eerie. Paul Morrow was walking about doing arm swing exercises.

Sandra pulled off a heavy gauntlet to operate the monitor gear. It read, POWER LOSS RATE 45%. She shoved down the stud and got for her trouble, POWER LOSS RATE 47%.

Morrow stopped his Swedish drill and used the PA net.

'*Attention all sections, Alpha. Phase Six power cuts now operative.*'

For the most part, his face on the communications posts was talking to empty and dimly lit areas. He went on, '*All Alphan experimental sections are closing down. Personnel are in-*

structed to evacuate immediately. Heating now automatically reduced to schedule two. That includes Medical.'

He put a hand on Sandra's shoulder. She was silent. It had to be. There was more, *'Travel tube facilities cancelled throughout Alpha. Effective as of now.'*

That caught some of the evacuees moving from closing sectors. Doors that had begun to open slid back to fail safe and the migrants were faced with a long circuitous trek through darkened corridors. More than anything yet it added to the sense of a gathering doom.

Except for Anna and Luke who were holding hands in the rumble there was not much more cheer on Eagle One. Alan Carter called 'Radio contact with Alpha imminent, Commander'.

Koenig left his seat beside Helena and went through to be ready and waiting.

Bob Mathias went on foot to Main Mission to sort it out with the top hand. There was an angry rasp in his voice as he said, 'What the hell is going on, Morrow?'

'There is nothing I can do.'

'If you maintain those cuts, you might as well shoot my patients.'

'All right, Doctor. I'm telling you there's no way we can give you back that power.'

'God dammit, they're sick people! They won't survive at those temperatures!'

'Then I can tell you, they'll be a little way ahead of the rest of us. If these power losses continue . . . *none* of us will survive.'

He held Mathias's angry glare for a beat. Mathias spun on his heel. At the hatch, he called out, 'It's on your conscience then, Morrow.'

Sandra tried the monitor. It read POWER LOSS RATE 50%.

Koenig's voice sounded on the Eagle Command net. 'Come in Main Mission.'

It was poor reception and Koenig's face on the screen was distorting.

'This is John Koenig. Do you read me?'

Morrow called, 'We have you, Eagle One.'

'Situation, Paul?'

'Fifty per cent power loss.'

'Listen carefully. We're clearing out. Put Operation Exodus into effect, immediately. Details later.'

Calculations raced through Morrow's head. Without normal power, it would be a mammoth task. Other staff were doing the sums. Grim faced, they watched him hit the PA button.

'This is Controller Paul Morrow. Stand by for an important announcement. We are putting Operation Exodus into immediate effect.'

Sandra Benes checked the monitor. It told her again, POWER LOSS RATE 50%. She cleared the screen and went through the sequence for confirmation.

Once more the screen glowed with POWER LOSS RATE 50%. She called, 'Paul!'

'What is it?'

'Look ... it's stopped. Power has stabilized.'

Disbelieving, Morrow checked the sequence for himself. She was right. He got it again, POWER LOSS RATE 50%.

He called, 'Kano. Computer check!'

As Kano moved, Morrow called Eagle One 'Commander. Something new. Power seems to have stabilized.'

Koenig's face was clearer. 'Stabilized? Are you sure?'

Computer print-out was coming off the press and Kano read it out, 'Computer confirms power loss, fifty per cent and stable.'

Morrow said, 'That's it, Commander, we're not losing any more power. It's holding at that. What about Exodus – do we go ahead?'

'Hold everything. Keep it on ice – if that isn't a dirty word. Wait until we get back.'

The first sign of a break in the all round gloom, it had Helena Russell and Bergman smiling at each other. Surely there was something they could work out? But the pair in the back seat took it another way. Faces grim, they looked at each other. Evacuation to Arkadia was no longer a sure thing.

As Eagle One dropped to her pad and a boarding tube ran out, Morrow made a welcome announcement, *'Phase Six power cuts cancelled. All other economies still stand.'*

It was a long walk to Main Mission. Koenig was still trying to think the thing through. He said, 'Helena, check out the survival requirements for the base on the terms of a fifty per cent power loss. Rush it through.'

Two by two, they were peeling off the group as they came to intersections. Left alone with Bergman, Koenig stopped at a communications post. 'What now, Paul?'

'Still fifty per cent and holding.'

'Do the instruments tell us anything?'

'Not the how or why, but it looks like it has really stabilized.'

Bergman was due to turn off for his section, 'The planetary data . . . do you want me to work on it?'

'Store it for now. When we have time we'll process it.'

Koenig walked on and stopped at the next post, 'Paul, check the energy requirements for high priority areas.'

'That's been done, Commander. We've just enough to keep them operational. Just.'

When he reached Main Mission, he was welcome. He could see from their faces that they expected him to pull something out of the hat.

'How does it go?'

Sandra pointed to her monitor, 'No change.'

'Good. Paul, I'd like a talk.'

In the command office, Koenig sank wearily into his command seat. It was wholly cold and cheerless. He said, 'Morale?'

'Not good. They've worked it out for themselves. They know we're stuck here. They know the power situation. They don't know why or how long this will last.'

'Priority one is to keep personnel alive.'

'What's the planet like?'

'Worse.'

The command console bleeped and Helena Russell's face joined the wake. But she had reasonably good news. 'John, if we hold at fifty per cent we have a viable system on food and life support. Not pleasant, but we could survive.'

Koenig came to a decision. 'Paul, call all sections. Cancel Exodus.'

Anna and Luke had gone straight to the reference library and were close together in one dimly lit alcove. Anna was speaking in muted tones like an entranced Sybil. 'Neither past nor future. The future is the past and the Testament of Arkadia is the link. They spoke to us . . . and we understood. Just you and I, Luke. There is no mistake.'

Their eyes linked and gently Luke raised her hands and kissed the palms.

'Yes. The time is now. We will do what has to be done.'

Morrow's announcement broke in, '*Attention all Sections Alpha. Operation Exodus is cancelled. Report for normal duties.*'

Luke stood up and drew Anna to her feet. Hand in hand they went to look for Koenig.

He was still sitting at his desk, too weary to move. When they came through the hatch, years of command experience told him he had labour trouble.

Anna went right to the point, 'Commander, we want to live on that planet.'

Rested and fresh, he might have had more tact. In the event, he said flatly, 'That's out of the question.'

Luke's hands clenched. If there had been a Kendo stick handy, he would have been beating at Koenig's head to let in a little light. 'We belong there. We were *guided* to that planet.'

Koenig said, 'Listen to me, Luke. Up here we have a chance, a chance we can measure. Down there, none at all.'

More gently, Anna pressed the case, 'But a few of us could survive on that planet. We could . . . Luke and I.'

'Surely you could – if you took half the supplies and made life impossible for the rest of us. No, I'm sorry.'

Luke's eyes had a fanatical glitter, 'But we *must* go, Commander!'

Harshly, Koenig said, 'You will do as I say. There are enough problems.'

There was a momentary hesitation then both turned as one and marched out into Main Mission. No speech was needed between them. Anna went on and left by the main hatch. Luke Ferro walked over to the computer desk. Pressing buttons he began a sequence, took notes and then edged over to Kano, getting himself between Kano and the rest of the staff. When Kano looked up he was staring into the tube of a laser.

Luke leaned forward confidentially.

'The combination of the protein store . . . give it to me.'

'You'll never get away with this.'

'Tell me. I'll kill you and everybody here.'

It carried conviction. Slowly Kano tapped it out and Luke reached over to rip off the print-out for himself. When it was in his hand, he took out his comlock and Anna's face appeared on the miniature screen. Quietly he spoke out the figure sequence and heard her say, 'Check.'

Then she was away, drawing her laser and thumbing the selector to STUN. At the protein store hatch, two security men smiled in greeting. Her hand came from behind her back and stun beams cracked over the gap. As they fell, she had her comlock out and was opening the door. Inside, there was an issue counter and behind it the locked panel. Working with the number sequence that Luke had relayed, she played the combination. She was through. She opened her comlock and said, 'Combination correct.'

Luke Ferro straightened up. Kano took his chance and hit a button. The general alarm went off with a mind bending din that had every operator leaping from his desk. The laser swept down in a savage arc and Kano crumpled over his console.

Koenig appeared at the top of the steps and stopped as the laser swung to cover him. Ferro backed off a step at a time towards the main hatch. Conveniently, it was opened for him. Helena Russell, coming in at a run, was level with him before she realised there was a heist.

It was a bonus for Luke Ferro. Quick as a flash, he had an arm round her waist and the laser jammed in the side of her neck. He had Koenig over a barrel. The expression on his face was enough. Koenig had moved, but stopped again. He said, 'You must be out of your mind, Ferro, put that laser away.'

He was moving forward to take it. Ferro warned, 'That's far enough. I'll kill her!'

There was a stop. 'Now, Commander. Will you give me what I ask?'

Humouring a madman, Koenig said, quietly, 'All right — an Eagle. Fuelled and ready to take off, but first release Doctor Russell.'

'You'll do as *I* say, Koenig! Do you hear me? What *I* say.'

Alan Carter ran in with Irwin and N'Dole at his heels. Ferro slewed half round to let them see what was happening. They stopped, looking at Koenig for guidance. N'Dole filled in some background. 'Commander, there's been a raid on the food stores . . . suspect Anna Davis . . . we're looking for her now.'

The pattern was all too clear. Ferro said savagely, 'Call them off!'

Irwin was sidling round to outflank Ferro and rush him from a blind quarter, but Koenig checked him. Luke Ferro recognised it as another tactical victory and grated out, 'Do it, Koenig!'

Making his movements plain, John Koenig walked deliberately to the communications post and hit the PA button. 'Security. Hold fast on the search.'

Turning to Ferro he went on, 'Okay. An Eagle. What else?'

'A moonbuggy. Stores and supplies to last us three years.'

Reaction from all hands was immediate and horrified. They looked at Koenig for a refusal. He said, 'Be rational. You know the problem. Do you realise what the loss of those supplies would do to us?'

'Your choice, Koenig. You'll do it or she'll die *and* you before they get to me.'

The hostage spoke up, 'You can't even consider it, John!'

He ignored her, 'Ferro, you realise you'll have no chance down on the planet . . . it's barren, a dead world.'

'No, Koenig,' it was a fanatic speaking. 'Not dead. *Dormant*. Waiting for life, waiting for us.'

Bergman tried. 'If we agree to your demands, you are condemning Alpha, all of us, to certain death.'

'If Alpha is to be the sacrificial lamb, let it be! I speak for a higher destiny. The Testament of Arkadia. Preordained from the moment the first Arkadian stepped out onto Earth. Don't you understand yet? What we shall do gives meaning to all the suffering of the Moon's long odyssey. What we were seeking has been found. No *accident* brought us to this planet, but divine ordination. The seed of life is carried back to its ancient place of origin.'

All eyes were on Koenig. They were convinced that he had a madman to deal with. His quiet reply took them aback.

'All right.'

Helena was appalled. Emotionally, she said, 'John! Don't let your feelings for me influence you. You must do what is right. No one life is worth what he asks.'

Again, he ignored her, 'I said it's a deal, Ferro.'

No one wanted Helena dead, but they reckoned she had stated the case. Anna Davis, rushing in with a laser in her hand, broke a stunned silence.

Koenig went further, 'Paul, order the stores and provisions – stow them in an Eagle. Alan, prepare the Eagle for launch.'

Nobody moved. Koenig's voice was a whiplash, 'Do it!'

The habit of taking his command was too strong. Both men went to work.

Luke Ferro said, 'We're moving to the launch pad now. Be warned. Any attempt to stop us will fail and bring down upon you the terrible forces of chaos and destruction.'

Irwin and N'Dole made to follow as the trio went out. Koenig said, 'Leave them. Irwin, a word with you.' He was a minute speaking quietly to the security man and then Irwin walked out. He left a highly charged silence. Koenig had made hard decisions in the past; but this time, they reckoned he had condemned them all on a personal issue.

They watched Ferro's party move through the base to a boarding exit. Morrow's voice was icy as he reported, 'The supplies are loaded on the Eagle.'

He got a nod from Koenig.

Even Victor Bergman was critical, 'Those supplies are vital to us, John; regardless of whose life is forfeit. That must include Helena's.'

'Don't you think I know that, Victor!'

Paul Morrow said, 'But we're just letting them walk away, Commander!'

'Luke Ferro is not holding a bible. It's a lethal weapon and he's obsessed. There's another point you overlook. The forces that stopped the Moon and cut the power are involved in some way we don't understand. If we make a false move, he'll wreck this base. Sandra, where are they now?'

'Approaching boarding area four.'

Koenig nodded, signalled to Bergman and N'Dole to follow and went out. Paul Morrow watched his withdrawing back and thumped viciously at his console.

The boarding tube was waiting. Anna Davis shepherded Helena inside and Luke Ferro followed slowly, watching Carter who was standing by. He asked, 'Is the Eagle ready to go, Carter?'

'When the ship's sinking, the rats are first to leave.'

'Keep clear.'

The boarding tube whipped away and homed on the entry hatch of the waiting Eagle. Inside the passenger module, crated stores took up most of the space. Anna kept Helena covered and Luke went through to the command module. He checked the panel. Fuel gauges showed maximum. He was a couple of minutes running through the console. Satisfied that he had a working ship, he prepared for lift-off.

Koenig and his party reached the boarding tube exit. Carter was still there and answered the unspoken question. 'They're inside.'

Koenig used his comlock. 'Ferro!'

Luke Ferro's face appeared on the miniature screen. 'Ferro, we did what you asked. Release Doctor Russell.'

'Not yet, Commander.'

'Release her, Ferro. We've kept our side of the bargain.'

'Doctor Russell comes with us.'

'Ferro. It isn't too late to blast that Eagle on its pad.'

'Don't do that, Commander. We won't harm her, you have my word.'

Carter put in, 'For what it's worth!'

Ferro went on. 'This is what you'll do. Escort us out into space. Use an unarmed reconnaissance Eagle. When we're out of range *then* you can have her back.'

Koenig looked beaten. He said harshly, 'Alan do as he says. Take reconnaissance Eagle Two and go with them.'

Bergman made a last try for reason, 'There's still time, Luke. Release Doctor Russell, hand over your weapons. There's still a place for you here.'

'There will be no more argument. I do what I must do.' Ferro switched himself off the link.

Koenig returned to Main Mission and an atmosphere that would cut with a knife. Morrow master-minded the Eagle take off. Formally he said, 'They're ready for lift off, *sir*.'

Luke's face came on the command set, dark and fanatical. 'Koenig. Any sign of pursuit and Dr Russell dies.'

Choking down a rising tide of fury, Koenig said, 'Understood.' He also spelled it out for Morrow.

'Controller, there will be no pursuit.'

Ferro's Eagle swept from the pad. Paul Morrow went through the drills to clear the escort. Every precise action was a clear indicator of his reading of the situation. Finally he said, 'That's it, Alan. Reconnaissance Eagle clear for take off.'

Carter said, savagely, 'Check. I'm on my way!' It was all too clear he would have preferred an armed craft and a mission to seek and intercept.

Moonbase Alpha settled to wait. Grim faced, Koenig sat at his command desk in a new and unwelcome isolation.

Luke Ferro in the command module of Eagle Four, saw Arkadia filling the screen of his scanner and shoved the controls on auto pilot. He went through to the passenger module and Anna smiled at him. They were home and dry. They could be generous.

Anna said, 'Doctor, we're truly sorry about this . . .'

'Sorry! What kind of word is that? You're killing three hundred people.'

Luke said, 'Will they die, Doctor? Do we know that? Why was the Moon stopped in space? Why was the power cut with no technical reason?'

'There is no explanation.'

'Isn't there? When the wheel of Destiny comes full circle – the tools it uses have their own logic. Isn't that so?'

She looked from one to the other. They were not criminals. They were crazy or inspired. She tried to reason, 'Listen to me, both of you. Physically, maybe you could survive down there. But have you thought what it will be like? You will be the only living beings on that barren planet. You're going to almost certain destruction.'

It was not the way they saw it. Their smiles as they looked at each other showed a naive and ingenuous trust. Luke said, 'No, Doctor. We're going home.'

John Koenig had moved to a direct vision port and was looking out at the starmap. Morrow called him and he returned to his desk, 'We've tracked them on optical, Commander. They're just about going into orbit.'

'Let me know the minute we have radio contact with Carter.'

At the same moment of time, out of range of the reduced power of the probes, Alan Carter was getting his first signal from Eagle Four. Luke Ferro's face appeared on his screen. 'Carter?'

'The same.'

'Stand by for docking. It's time to part company.'

Eagle Four eased in flight and Carter manoeuvred alongside. A boarding tube snaked over the ten metre gap and clamped home.

Helena Russell paused at the hatch. The two looked suddenly vulnerable and alone. On an impulse, she came forward, embraced them both and then turned on her heel to join Carter. As the hatch sliced shut at her back, they stood hand in hand, waited for the green tell-tale to indicate that the boarding tube had been retracted and then walked through to the command module to strap in for the home run.

The Reconnaissance Eagle wheeled away and headed back. When Sandra picked it up at the extreme of her shortened range she alerted Morrow and he called the outcast in the command office. Koenig could be seen sitting at his desk looking in front, tapping one finger on the housing of his console.

Paul Morrow said, 'We'll have voice contact with Carter in thirty seconds, Commander.'

Koenig was on his feet and using his comlock to open the hatch into Main Mission. He was standing behind Morrow's chair when Alan Carter's voice, laced with static, crackled on the Eagle Command net.

'Calling Alpha. Reconnaissance Eagle heading for Alpha. Do you read me?'

Koenig reached over and took the link. 'Koenig . . . Helena?'

'Safe. With me. We've lost Eagle Four.'

So the trade had been carried through. Koenig had sold them down the river. Morrow's voice was bitter, 'What now, Commander?'

Koenig was calling again, 'Technical?'

'Technical Section here, Commander.'

'Did you do what I asked?'

'No problem, Commander. It's on sub space frequency two, two, zero . . .'

'Well done.' He shifted to the Eagle Command net. 'Pursuit Eagle Three?'

'Commander?'

'Switch to sub space frequency two, two, zero.'

'Two, two, zero. Check, Commander.'

'Pursuit Eagle Five?'

'Eagle Five.'

'Switch to sub space frequency two, two, zero.'

There was interest all round. It was still cold and gloomy in Main Mission, but there was a feeling that they were in business again. Bergman was on to it first. He said, 'Dammit, John. You've put a trace on that ship.'

Koenig said, 'Activate,' and a low pulsing signal sounded out. He turned to Morrow. 'Right, Paul. Get those supplies back.'

There was a snag, Paul Morrow said, 'But, Commander, they'll be on the surface before the pursuit Eagles can catch up. It's vast. They'll never find them.'

'The trace is not on the Eagle, it's on the moonbuggy. You'll find them wherever they are. Now get those Eagles away.'

Main Mission swung behind its Controller with a will. For one thing it was a way to show that they regretted the failure in trust. Minutes later, Paul Morrow could report the all clear from the pads. He said formally, 'Pursuit Eagles Three and Five ready for launch, Commander.'

As if on cue, Main Mission took a sickening lurch that sent personnel reeling in all directions and turned the orderly desks into instant chaos.

Clawing a way back to his seat, Paul Morrow looked at his console. His shout cut through the hubbub, 'Commander . . . we're moving again.'

Only a few seconds behind him, Sandra Benes had reached her own work head. The power monitor stared at her and she took a new reading. The legend repeated, POWER LOSS RATE 47%.

She called, 'The *power*! We're gaining power!'

Koenig looked at Bergman. It made no sense. He snapped out, 'Abort the mission, Paul!'

'But the supplies?'

'With power coming back, we have the means to restock.'

Bergman thought of something else, 'The Reconnaissance Eagle!'

Koenig hit a button, 'Carter. This is an emergency. Hurry it along. Alpha's on the move again. Hit that drive or you'll get left in the outback.'

'Check, Commander!'

The Reconnaissance Eagle surged forward as though booted up the rudder by a cosmic foot.

Arkadia was feeling the effect of the Moon's surge forward. A driving wind whipped up and ran blindly over the unpeopled wastes. Luke Ferro saw the outriders of the storm and dropped the crate he was carrying. It burst open and yellow seed spilled out to cover his feet.

But he ignored it. He was staring, transfixed, at the huge

bowl of the sky. Their late home was on the move. He yelled, 'Anna!'

She came running. Together, they watched Earth's Moon diminish to a dot.

Soberly, as if waking from a dream, they looked at each other. The full impact of their isolation was breaking through. The first probing fingers of the sighing wind plucked at their clothing. Overwhelmed, Anna sobbed in sudden fear.

Luke Ferro drew her close and held her shaking body. All they had was each other. It could be enough. It would have to be enough. For that matter, it was all there ever was anywhere, a man and a woman trying to make sense of the human situation.

The wind lifted the seed and scattered it over the barren land.

Koenig was at the entry port when Alan Carter and Helena stepped through. Knowing when he was not wanted, Carter lifted a gauntlet in greeting and walked off.

Hands outstretched Koenig went to meet her. The lights had gone on in Moonbase Alpha, but without her it would be an empty shell. He had put it all in the balance against her safety, but he could not regret it. Maybe it disqualified him from the command slot?

He said, 'All right?'

'Yes, I'm fine.'

Her blonde hair against his cheek, she said, 'They're all alone down there, John.'

He could still feel angry about that, 'That's right and there's nothing we can do about it. It was their choice.'

'Was it their choice? I believe they were possessed.'

The Moon fled on. Arkadia diminished to a speck and winked out beyond the range of the probes. Koenig sat late in his command office bringing the log up to date.

Dictating into the recorder, he said, 'Now that Alpha is safe, we can only wonder at the forces which almost destroyed us. On reflection, we must ask if we were right to resist Luke Ferro and Anna Davis in their almost inspired need to take the gift of life back to a dead world. Had not our fight been for immediate survival we might not have failed to understand the transcendental nature of their act.'

He paused and looked out at the black velvet starmap and the infinite scatter of stars. There had to be one. Somewhere, there had to be one Ithaca. He signed off, 'Meanwhile our search for a home continues.'

He stood up. Meanwhile, also, he would go and see how his particular Penelope was faring.

BEFORE THE GOLDEN AGE 1

Isaac Asimov

For many s.f. addicts the Golden Age began in 1938 when John Campbell became editor of Astounding Stories. For Isaac Asimov, the formative and most memorable period came in the decade before the Golden Age – the 1930s. It is to the writers of this generation that BEFORE THE GOLDEN AGE is dedicated.

Some – Jack Williamson, Murray Leinster, Stanley Weinbaum and Asimov himself – have remained famous to this day. Others such as Neil Jones, S. P. Meek and Charles Tanner, have been deservedly rescued from oblivion.

BEFORE THE GOLDEN AGE was originally published in the United States in a single mammoth volume of almost 1,200 pages. The British paperback edition will appear in four books, the first of which covers the years 1930 to 1933.

BEFORE THE GOLDEN AGE 3

Isaac Asimov

In this third volume, Isaac Asimov has selected a feast of rousing tales such as BORN BY THE SUN by Jack Williamson, with its marvellous vision of the solar system as a giant incubator; Murray Leinster's story of parallel time-tracks SIDEWISE IN TIME; and Raymond Z. Gallin's OLD FAITHFUL which features one of science fiction's most memorable aliens – Number 774.

'Sheer nostalgic delight ... stories by authors long-forgotten mingle with those by ones who are well-known, and still writing. A goldmine for anyone interested in the evolution of s.f.'
Sunday Times

'Contains some of the very best s.f. from the Thirties ... emphatically value for money.'
Evening Standard

A MIDSUMMER TEMPEST

Poul Anderson

'The best writing he's done in years ... his language is superb. Worth buying for your permanent collection.'
– *The Alien Critic*

Somewhere, spinning through another universe, is an Earth where a twist of fate, a revolution and a few early inventions have made a world quite unlike our own.

It is a world where Cavaliers and Puritans battle with the aid of observation balloons and steam trains; where Oberon and Titania join forces with King Arthur to resist the Industrial Revolution; and where the future meshes with the past in the shape of Valeria, time traveller from New York.